MORE BOOKS BY JIM KJELGAARD

Big Red	Stormy
Irish Red	Desert Dog
Outlaw Red	Snow Dog
Haunt Fox	Rebel Siege
Lion Hound	Wild Trek
Forest Patrol	Fire-Hunter
Kalak of the Ice	Trailing Trouble
Buckskin Brigade	A Nose for Trouble
Wolf Brother	Chip, the Dam Builder
Hidden Trail	Wildlife Cameraman

BOOMERANG HUNTER

Boomerang HUNTER

BY JIM KJELGAARD

ILLUSTRATED BY W. T. MARS

HOLIDAY HOUSE, NEW YORK, N.Y.

THIRD PRINTING
COPYRIGHT, 1960, BY EDNA KJELGAARD. PRINTED IN U.S.A.

TABLE OF CONTENTS

CHAPTER ONE

When he came out on the ledge that overlooked the water hole, Balulu shifted his boomerang to his left hand and squatted on his haunches. His tame, dog-like dingo, Warrigal, padded silently forward and crouched beside him. Balulu let his right hand rest on the big red dingo's furry neck and breathed a silent thanks. Most of the Desert People's tame dingoes had already gone to the cooking fires, and the few that remained to the tribe would not long escape the same fate. The finest of hunting dogs were valueless when there was so little to hunt, and even when the eyes saw some tame dingo as a valued hunting companion, the hungry belly that saw it as food presented a more powerful argument. But eating the remaining dingoes was no solution, Balulu realized; the Desert People desperately needed to find a new supply of game, and soon. Otherwise, the tribe would starve.

Balulu stared intently at the water hole, one of the very few not yet drunk up by the Devil Who Lived Where the River Had Flowed. This and three similar water holes marked a rough triangle to which the Desert People had been restricted for the past seven seasons. If there was little game to be found near them now, there was even less elsewhere.

His gaze fixed on the water hole, Balulu tightened his grip on Warrigal and thought back to previous hunts. From the maturity of his fifteen years he remembered clearly that, a mere three years ago, the water hole into which he now looked had been hidden by the river. The scrub in the parched valley that now stretched before him had been green, not gray. Rather than dust flats and withered vegetation, there had been grass and succulent plants on both sides of the river. So many big kangaroos came to feed in the meadows then that even unskilled hunters were able to kill them. For the tribe's Senior Hunters, it was child's play.

Balulu thought about his first kangaroo hunt, when he had been but a stripling, and Warrigal an eight-month-old puppy with much to learn about the art of hunting.

Led by Morula, the Senior Hunters had stolen forth and concealed themselves in the scrub. Balulu and the other youths who hoped to become Senior Hunters, aided by the women and children, had driven the feeding kangaroos toward the ambushed spearsmen.

Such a hunt, with those of greater experience hidden in a manner that would enable them to make the most effective use of spears and boomerangs, and the rest chivvying game toward them, was time-tested and approved. As the kangaroos turned in alarm from the weapons of the Senior Hunters, the youths closed in, hoping to make kills of their own. That is how Balulu had killed his first full-grown kangaroo, a great red male.

That had been three summers ago, and it was their last great feast. Remembering it now, Balulu licked his lips longingly. Then the Desert People used to live from season to season, wandering from water hole to water hole, taking game as they pleased. Now they lived from day to day, searching ceaselessly for game that became ever scarcer.

The Devil Who Lived Where the River Had Flowed had brought the change about. So said Loorola, the tribe's Witch Doctor. In any event, Balulu knew that the river had flowed, at varying levels, since the oldest member of the Desert People could remember. As long as there was enough water, there had been no lack of game for the men to hunt or roots for the women to dig. Though individual members of the tribe had known spear-pierced bellies, devil-haunted bellies, or food-rejecting bellies, those able to eat had seldom known a hungry belly.

All that had been before the Devil drank up the whole river. Thereafter, said Loorola, the Devil gained control of the sky, from which he allowed no rain to fall. Deprived of water, the grasses shriveled and many of the edible roots died. When there was no more to eat, birds and beasts that had once abounded either starved to death or went elsewhere. Perhaps the Devil had taken them away.

Only the wild dingoes, once-proud beasts that had become as miserable and humbled as the surviving members of the tribe, remained in any number. They ringed every night's camp, dogged anyone who ventured forth for any reason, followed every march when camps were changed, and snatched anything they could whenever they were able to get it.

Balulu turned to glance at the pack that was following him and Warrigal. There were seven of the beasts, so lean-flanked and slat-ribbed that their heads seemed grotesquely large in comparison to shrunken bodies. They had been on the trail of Balulu and Warrigal since early this morning, hoping to catch Balulu off guard, or to steal anything he was unable to carry away if he made a kill. At no time had they come within range of

Balulu's boomerang, and now they were waiting just beyond such range.

That was how they acted during the day, but woe betide anyone caught away from a protecting fire at night. The emaciated dingoes were as swift and deadly by darkness as they ever were in full sunlight, and at night the advantage was theirs. No member of the tribe who left his night fire did so without a weapon in hand.

Balulu paid little attention to the pack. The wild dingoes might come within easy spear range, and they would still be safe from him.

The last survivor of the Dingo Totem in his tribe, he had even been denied the morsel of meat that might have been his share when the Desert People started eating their tame dingoes. Wild or tame, Balulu could neither kill nor eat a dingo, for they were his sworn brothers and in the body of one of them lived his other self. If he killed a dingo it was even possible that he would be killing himself, for if his life had no place to go when it took leave of his body, it must perish too.

Looking east across the Australian desert, Balulu saw a faint intermingling of shadows. Actually the shadows were mountains where, in former happy times, the Desert People had hunted for a part of every year. They used to go to the mountains when the mali was in bloom, showing that the hot summer was approaching, and stay in the highlands until the killing frosts came.

For the past two summers, however, they had not gone to their usual haunts in the mountains. Every sprig of vegetation in the high country lived by rainfall, so the mountains were hardest hit by drought. Only the greatest and most deeply rooted trees, such as the sky-piercing eucalyptus, retained any leaves at all and even those were shriveled. The smaller trees and shrubs rattled naked branches to every wind that blew. Once-lush patches of grass had become mere playgrounds for dust devils. The highland water holes had turned to slime-covered puddles, then to bowls of dried, cracked mud. The tribe no longer went to the mountains because there was no hope there. One might deny a hungry belly, but he must have water or die.

Conditioned by ages of aridity, the desert had fared somewhat better than the mountains. But even the hardiest of desert plants need some water, and the drought had levied an enormous tribute.

Balulu stared at the mountains, and thought about the Devil Who Lived Where the River Had Flowed. Did he rule everywhere, as Loorola said, and were all living things doomed? Or was there a far place beyond the Devil's power, where rivers still flowed and game was plentiful?

Balulu had given much thought to the Devil of late. Was it real, or was it just something that Loorola had made up to conceal his own waning powers? A good witch doctor should be able to make rain when it was needed, but it was plain that Loorola could no longer do so, for whatever reason.

Turning back to the water hole, Balulu became instantly aware that there had been a change within the past few seconds, since the last time he'd looked. The slender, four-foot outline resembled a shadow, but it was not a shadow. It had a lizard's shape and lizards were good to eat. Boomerang in one hand and spears in the other, Balulu backed quietly away from the front of the ledge. Knowing game had been sighted, Warrigal paced beside him. Once out of sight of the lizard, Balulu ran down the sloping end of the ledge and cautiously approached the spot where he had seen the saurian. There was a cluster of boulders here, and Balulu kept behind the largest as he advanced in a crouch, his bare feet soundless on the hot, dry sand. Warrigal slunk at his heels.

Laying down all his weapons but his two throwing spears, Balulu took one in each hand and peered around the boulder. The lizard had not moved. In one motion Balulu drew back his arm and threw. The slender, stone-tipped shaft flew true, transfixing the lizard just back of the front legs. In three strides Balulu was on the thrashing saurian, had thrust his second spear through the neck, and pinned it to the ground.

Snarling and snapping, Warrigal rushed up, but there was no need for the dingo's help. The lizard was dead. Balulu shouldered his prize, retrieved the rest of his weapons, and headed back to the tribe.

The Desert People were camped in a swale that was sheltered from night winds and was almost unobstructed by boulders or vegetation. The open camp was a point which was never neglected now; if the wild dingoes attacked they would be sighted in ample time. Looking down from the rim of the swale, Balulu saw the tribes people clustered about fires and smelled roasting meat. His heart turned cold.

In the days when hunting had been good, every hunter had kept at least one tame dingo to assist in the chase and some had whole packs. This morning, when Balulu left, there had still been six hunting dingoes in camp. Now there were only four, and the smell of roasting meat explained itself. Balulu touched Warrigal's head.

"They shall never have you, my brother," he promised.

The dingo beside him, Balulu strode into camp and pretended not to see the many hungry glances that were directed at him. He went straight to a sizable boulder, the only one in camp, and laid his game beside it with the head pointing at the sacred mark that Loorola had inscribed on the boulder.

Stooping, Balulu used his flint-headed stabbing stick to cut as much meat as he needed for Warrigal and himself.

This stabbing stick was Balulu's particular pride, for its flint head was the only one in the tribe, and far keener of edge than the chipped-stone heads the Desert People used to tip their throwing spears. His father had traded for it with a wandering hunter from a tribe far to the north, years ago, and it had become Balulu's when his father had been killed in a fight with the Mountain People.

Leaving the rest of the lizard, which automatically became community property after the successful hunter had his choice, Balulu went to the little depression near which he slept and blew dead ashes from the cooking fire there.

He laid dry twigs on the hot coals that were exposed, then divided the lizard meat into two equal piles and let Warrigal choose. The dingo gulped his portion raw, but Balulu cooked his in the hot sand and ashes. Then he went to sleep with Warrigal's furry body for a pillow. The last thing he was aware of was the moaning of wild dingoes, already coming nearer camp as dusk thickened.

At break of day, a man got up and went to the fire that Balulu had used last night. He poked among the still-smouldering embers with a saltbrush withe that had burned partly through. The charred end scraped harshly in the morning stillness, and at this indication that life was stirring in camp, the dingoes out in the scrub began an excited whimper.

Balulu, who never slept so soundly that he did not know subconsciously what was going on, came to full wakefulness when the man rose. Balulu saw who it was who had arisen. Rono, leader of the tribe and proud wearer of the emu plume, hoped to find some morsel of food that Balulu had overlooked last night. As he poked about the fire, he was not Rono alone, he was any member of the tribe. But was the desperate hope he expressed worthy of a leader? Balulu felt a sudden contempt.

Rono had become leader after Morula grew too old, though it was true that he had become so only because nobody among the remaining Senior Hunters felt equal to challenging his claim. Rono was still leader, and as such he was theoretical ruler of everyone in the tribe except the few old grandmothers who remained alive. The grandmothers feared no one, and chief or anyone who asserted domination over them was sure to feel their tart tongues.

A little wind rippled the emu plume Rono wore in his hair. No petty mark of distinction, that plume must be plucked, while competent witnesses observed, from a full-grown and unwounded bird. Such an achievement was far from trivial. First one must approach near enough to pluck a plume, and emus, although they could not fly, could run like the wind. Furthermore, an adult emu, standing nearly as tall as a man, could, and often did, inflict dangerous wounds with its powerful, three-toed feet. Of all who aspired to wear the coveted plume, only the bravest won that mighty honor.

Balulu stirred uneasily. It ill befitted a wearer of the emu plume to poke in a dying fire for food that was not there, like a scavenging kea parrot that flies after hunting dingoes in the hope of getting some offal. But Rono was by no means alone in doing things he never would have done if conditions were normal. The whole tribe was different.

It was a puzzling change that Balulu could not understand, but it certainly existed. Balulu knew only that the tribe was made up of people, and people had always been superior to animals. But when the river stopped flowing and the rain ceased to fall, the resulting famine somehow seemed to pull people down so that they were ever closer to animals. It was not a good thing, but Balulu could see no way to change it.

Suddenly, out in the scrub beyond the swale, a

red-furred dingo leaped high in the air, snapped
its jaws twice, and fell back to earth. Jumping up
and snatching a boomerang, Balulu raced toward
the place, Warrigal beside him. Rono, who had
also seen the dingo leap, was already running.
Rono held the saltbrush withe with which he had
been poking the fire, as he would have carried a
spear. There was no time to return to his fire for a
proper weapon.

Both of the aborigines knew that, in full daylight, the camp-following dingoes would retreat
from two armed men. But first they'd try to tear
apart and devour their fallen comrade. They must
not be permitted to do so; the tribe needed food
too desperately.

Rono had already reached and was looking
down at the fallen dingo when Balulu, still twenty yards away, identified the thing that had killed
it. The sluggish wind carried a sweet and sickish
odor that was like no other.

The scent was that of a black snake, a deadly
viper whose venom invariably brought death unless one was able to find and apply certain ground-

hugging herbs that defied even a black snake's poison. Nor was there ever much time in which to find the herbs. Most things that felt a black snake's fangs died soon afterwards. Some lived only seconds, but usually these ran afoul of big snakes with a great store of venom. From the speed with which the dingo had died, this snake must be a monster. Dingoes, even when half-starved, did not die easily, although it was not unusual for one to fall to a black snake.

Coming up to the dead dingo, Balulu stopped, looked, and threw his boomerang. It arced gracefully into the scrub, and a clump of grass began to shake violently as the snake went into its death throes.

Rono looked around. "What for?" he demanded angrily.

"I am of the Dingo Totem," Balulu reminded him. "The snake killed a dingo, my wild brother. I have avenged his death."

"It might have killed another dingo," grumbled Rono, "and so provided us more food."

"In thinking of his belly, Rono forgets his lore,"

Balulu said disdainfully. "Who waits to eat until black snakes kill dingoes for him, will have a pinched belly."

"That is true," Rono conceded reluctantly, "but the wild dingoes have become very wary and are hard to come near enough to kill."

"The snake is food now," Balulu pointed out.

"Yes," Rono agreed. "The snake is food now."

They caught up the dead dingo and the dead snake and started back to camp.

CHAPTER TWO

A half hour before the first gray streak of morning cracked the night sky's smooth black shell,
Balulu awoke and sat up. For a moment he listened to the moaning of the wild dingoes out in
the scrub. Then he added fresh wood to his fire
and watched the tongues of yellow flame lick
greedily at the fresh fuel.

There was a rustle, a half-sensed clicking of
padded paws, and Warrigal was at his side. The
dingo had never been fawning in his relationship,
and recent events had created a widening chasm
between Warrigal and all humans except Balulu.
The bond between the two had steadily strength-

ened. When they hunted, Warrigal did not hesitate to strike off on his own and range as far as he
chose, and to rejoin Balulu when he thought best.
But in camp, or even in the presence of another
human, he was usually at Balulu's side.

It seemed to Balulu as though Warrigal understood this time of desperation and knew what it
was doing to humans and beasts alike. Whether or
not his brother dingo actually had such thoughts,
the mere fact that he seemed to have them gave
Balulu heart.

Patiently he waited for daylight; with the wild
dingoes in the scrub, it would be too dangerous to
venture out before that time. There would be no
morning meal for Warrigal and himself, but there
had been so many mornings, even days, without
food that one more could easily be faced. So
could the fact that they would be hungrier when
the day ended than they already were before it
started, if they failed in this day's hunt.

Presently Rono left his sleeping hollow and
came toward Balulu's fire. Warrigal bristled, and
his lips curled in a silent snarl. Balulu put a re-

straining hand on his neck. Until recently the big dingo had been friendly toward Rono; there must be something behind this sudden dislike. Balulu suspected that Rono, a hunter of vast experience, knew some secret means—perhaps a scent, or a plant or shrub—that stirred dingoes to resentment.

Balulu also knew there was a very good reason why Rono preferred hostility between Warrigal and himself. Rono was leader, therefore he was supreme. But his rule was entirely dependent on his ability to sustain it. Any tribesman who felt equal to so doing was entitled to challenge him, and the challenger automatically became chief if he won.

Balulu's skill with both boomerang and spear were well known throughout the Desert People. He suspected that Rono thought it wise to temper authority with judgment, lest Balulu challenge him. And he might well do so, if Rono ordered Warrigal surrendered for eating. But if the leader or anyone else were attacked by the dingo, not even Balulu could hold them responsible for defending themselves or blame them for killing Warrigal.

As Rono approached, Warrigal dropped to a half crouch and flexed his muscles for leaping. Balulu wrapped his fingers about a fistful of hair and clung tightly. If Rono had indeed set out to earn Warrigal's dislike, he had succeeded. Without Balulu to restrain his brother, the dingo would perhaps be at Rono's throat even now.

Naked except for the belt hanging about his middle, Rono came up to Balulu's fire. The flames reflecting from his body painted it a gleaming bronze-black, highlighted by the ceremonial totem scars on his chest and arms.

Warrigal snarled again, but, as though he did not hear, Rono made no move to indicate that he was even thinking of the big dingo. Balulu could not help a grudging admiration. Rono knew that Warrigal was aching to attack, and the very fact that he could stand without flinching spoke well for his courage. Balulu decided that Rono did not want an attack at this time, when there were no witnesses to testify that he had killed Warrigal justly, and was depending on Balulu to control the aroused dingo.

"You do not cook at your fire," Rono observed.

"You speak with the tongue of Old Man Who Has Lost His Wits," Balulu growled. "If I had meat, would not the tribe know it? Did I not share the lizard I left at Loorola's Rock of the Four Winds? Who else brought in meat?"

"I do not talk of such meat," Rono said. "Of the many hunters who were abroad yesterday, only Balulu made a kill. That is true. I talk of the meat that lies beside you, and that even now would wish to have its jaws tearing my throat."

For a short time, Balulu did not answer, but considered the meaning behind the leader's words. Evidently Rono had decided that Warrigal must be eaten. However, he had given not an order but a suggestion, carefully presented as such. So Balulu might disagree without flouting Rono's authority.

"There is wisdom in your words," Balulu said gravely. "Though I may not taste his flesh, my brother will indeed stay the hunger of those who are not of the Dingo Totem. I will give Warrigal to the cooking fires on one condition."

"Say the condition."

"Warrigal shall be spared until after the next emu is captured. The emu shall be brought in and made ready for eating. Rono himself shall have the first portion."

Suddenly raging, Rono snarled, "Your words are spear points! Have you forgotten that I am of the Emu Totem? How else dare you say such words?"

"The words sprang from your tongue to mine!" Balulu retorted. "When you proposed that I willingly surrender Warrigal to the cooking fires, had you forgotten that I am of the Dingo Totem?"

There was a brief silence during which Rono pondered the trap he had set for Balulu and the way it had been turned on himself. Who violated his pledges to his own totem was always despised by the tribe. But who caused another to betray his totem flouted the most sacred laws. His punishment, always decided by the Council of Elders, was invariably death.

"I meant no harm," Rono said shortly. "Good hunting."

"And to you," Balulu replied. "May fat and unwary game cross your path."

Rono turned on his heel and walked away. Relieved but uneasy, Balulu watched him go. Warrigal had now come to represent more than just food; in addition he symbolized Balulu's defiance of his leader. Rono would certainly try again.

The gathering day had become almost light enough for him to leave the safety of the night fires and set out on the hunt. Balulu forgot Rono and devoted himself to a ritual which he had observed every day since his father had placed the first toy weapons in his hand, and would continue to practice until the day of his death. He inspected his weapons and gear.

The entire collection was carefully arranged within easy reach but a safe distance from the fire. Representing all the earthly possessions he had ever had, ever wanted, or would ever need, all together weighed less than twenty pounds. It was not only enough, but any roving hunter would have been overburdened with more. There was a pouch made from a tanned kangaroo skin; fire sticks and bark tinder; two boomerangs; a length of cord spun from possum hair, that he usually carried wound around his head; his flint-headed stabbing stick that could be used for killing or skinning game; two long, slender spears with stone heads lashed to their tips; and a *womera*, or throwing stick.

Balulu looked first to his boomerangs, his favorite weapon. About two feet from curved tip to curved tip and tapered at both ends, both were heavy war weapons that would not return to the thrower's hand. There was a certain disadvantage in that since, once thrown, they were useless until recovered. For that reason, some hunters chose to carry one war boomerang and one of the lighter weapons that would fly back to the thrower.

Balulu preferred two heavy weapons because of their greater range and deadlier effect. The lighter ones would usually kill small game instantly and sometimes cripple big game, even the great red kangaroo, so that it could be run down and killed, but they were most practical for hunting small game only. War boomerangs could be used on game of any size with devastating effect. The more skilled marksmen, using a war boomerang in good light, could pinpoint their targets at considerable distances. Balulu was expert enough to knock a kea from its perch at a hundred yards.

The boomerangs in need of no attention, he laid them aside and took up his spears.

There was a general pattern for all weapons among the tribe's hunters, but one man's were never exactly like another's simply because everyone was his own craftsman. Spears, like everything else, were influenced by personal preference, skill, and the maker's ambition. Balulu had fashioned his spears with such painstaking care that Rono himself did not have finer weapons. They had served him well, and were apparently in need of no repairs. Balulu laid them near the boomerangs and took up his *womera*.

Made of wood, and laboriously fashioned to his personal taste, the spear thrower was about two feet over all. The grip was shaped to conform per-

fectly to the shape of Balulu's clenched fist. At the
tip end was a spear rest, a cavity made with a
burning brand and sand-polished to a glassy
smoothness. When in use, the butt end of the
spear rested in the cavity, and the *womera's* effect
was to double the length of a spearsman's arm
and permit a corresponding increase in the force
and effective range of the thrown spear.

His major weapons in satisfactory condition,
Balulu turned to his other equipment. He examined the hide lashing on the flint point of his stabbing stick, checked his fire sticks, his supply of
bark tinder, and the other contents of his pouch.
All seemed to be in order. His clothing was a matter of no concern whatever, for he wore nothing
but a hanging belt.

This inspection completed, with no repairs necessary, and the light grown strong enough for distance visibility, Balulu and Warrigal left camp. A
few of the other tribesmen were up and about,
but nobody else had as yet started out to hunt.
Even Rono seemed to share the general gloomy

mood that there was no game to be found and was sitting cross-legged, staring morosely at the Rock of the Four Winds.

The camp behind him, Balulu turned to see how many wild dingoes had fallen in on his trail. He saw five grizzled adults that were following just beyond the effective range of his boomerang. With no more thought for the wild dingoes, since their presence on his trail every time he left camp had long been taken for granted, Balulu started into the parched desert.

With no clear idea of any direction that might lead him to quarry, he guided himself by his long-standing rules of hunting. He moved against the wind so that whatever lay ahead could not scent him; he kept to the heights so that he would not overlook anything hidden in the gullies and washes, and he was constantly sensitive to Warrigal and what the big dingo was doing. There was always a possibility that Warrigal would be the first to detect anything.

There was no valid reason to travel in any particular direction with the thought that game would be found; these days luck alone brought the hunter to his quarry. But even though the chances for success were so slim, Balulu could not rid himself of a feeling that he was right and the discouraged hunters who chose to idle in camp were wrong. Even when game had been most abundant, it had been necessary to go hunt for it; wild animals had never been known to come seek the hunter. With their situation more desperate than it had ever before been, it seemed to Balulu that all hunters should be working harder than ever.

With the sun four hours high, Balulu had seen nothing except parched desert and the wild dingoes that followed him. Although he had no reason to expect there would be anything in this dry, dead world, as long as daylight lasted he intended to hunt.

After another empty hour, Balulu slipped beneath the rim of a steep ridge up which he had been traveling and squatted beside a huge boulder. Warrigal came to sit near him. Balulu glanced across the narrow gully beneath him and began to study the opposite slope.

A twin of the ridge he had been climbing, the opposite slope was heavy with tough brush and scrub that was either immune to drought or was tapping some sub-surface water. Curious, his eyes missing nothing, Balulu squatted on his haunches and carefully scanned the opposite rise.

He did not really expect to see anything because he had glimpsed nothing all day. He continued to study the scrub-grown slope only because there *might* be game in such a place. When he finally caught a flicker of motion in the scrub, he was not at once able to tell whether or not anything had actually moved. More than once eager hope had seen game where the senses found none.

Balulu riveted his eyes on the place where there might have been motion. Presently he gave an involuntary start. His eyes were not playing him tricks. An animal had indeed moved, but it was a creature which the most stout-hearted hunter would ordinarily avoid.

When it moved from the concealing scrub and

halted in a tiny clearing, Balulu saw clearly a
thylacine, or marsupial tiger. There was no mis-
taking the dark brown stripes running across the
rear half of its back. About the size of Warrigal's,
the lean body was a perfect frame for its owner's
ferocious temperament. Flesh-eating thylacines
were dreaded for their willingness to fight anything, anywhere, at any time, and when attacked
they were truly ferocious. Who challenged a thylacine must kill or be killed. Still, beneath its
striped coat the thylacine was flesh, and flesh
could be eaten. This was no time to shrink from
danger.

Balulu made his decision and threw his boomerang in the same split second. The spinning
weapon sailed across the gully, made its loop, and
struck precisely where it had been aimed. Its
skull cracked, the thylacine dropped in its tracks.

From out in the scrub came a hoarse, gutteral
bark, and was answered by another. The marsupial tigers almost never ran in packs but there had
been three in this one—four, Balulu realized with
a sinking heart, for still another thylacine now

raised its coughlike bark. Then the wind carried Balulu's scent to them and they started down the opposite slope, straight toward him.

Balulu shifted his second boomerang to his right hand and clutched his spears in his left as he and Warrigal braced themselves.

CHAPTER THREE

Though his legs had an almost overwhelming urge to turn and run, they were overruled by Balulu's judgment. Marsupial tigers were by no means the fleetest of creatures, but not even dingoes had more stamina or keener noses. In their relentless pursuit, thylacines could wear down even the fastest animals. Balulu knew that they could follow him by scent, and that once on his trail, they would never give up. Even though he might run away from them for a little while, sooner or later the thylacines would be at his heels and he would be forced to defend himself anyhow. It was wiser to fight now, when he was fresh instead of tired and while some advantage remained on his side. Since there was only one real choice, Balulu's legs became steady.

Ordinarily thylacines did not hunt men, only kangaroos and wallabies. Nor did they usually travel in pairs. The surliest and most evil-tempered of beasts, the marsupial tiger's way was a lonely one. Even mated pairs could not endure each other's company for very long, and the mother with weanling young was the only normal example of thylacines traveling together. The fact that these had banded together defied all the rules that Balulu knew. They were not mother and cubs, but four adults apparently driven by desperation to pool their strength. Where they had come from or how long they had wandered in this parched land Balulu did not know, but there was no doubt in his mind that their purpose in running as a pack was to find food. Nor was there any question that a half-starved thylacine would be far more dangerous than a well-fed one.

All this was clear to Balulu within a few seconds after discovering that he faced a pack. As soon as the tigers started down the slope and it became obvious that he and Warrigal must shortly fight for their lives, Balulu considered the best plan of defense.

The thylacine he had killed, and which at first he supposed was the only one, had been at almost the extreme range of his boomerang. He had known that when he threw, and had done so only because the beast had been in a clearing and perfectly still. With another boomerang and two throwing spears, Balulu had retained a comfortable reserve of strength against just one thylacine. Now he must meet three.

His second boomerang loosely gripped in his throwing hand, he watched the three thylacines race down the far slope. One, slightly faster, was somewhat ahead of the other two. All three were intent on the quarry they had scented, each one eager to be first at the kill. As though guided by an invisible signal, they sped up the wind current that carried the scents of the man and the dingo.

All three were in sight, but at no time did Balulu have an unobstructed look at any one. They were flitting images in the scrub, more or less easy to see as the growth grew thin or dense. Though they were much nearer than their pack mate had been when Balulu killed it, to throw his one remaining boomerang now would be to waste it. Not only was a running target infinitely more difficult than a stationary one, but the scrub would deflect a boomerang even if it were perfectly on target.

Balulu marked the spot where the foot of the far slope met the gully. Only scattered clumps of spinifex grass grew there, leaving nothing that might turn a boomerang. Though there were boulders on the floor of the gully, any boomerang that struck one would be a wild shot, far enough off target so that it would not have hit anyway. Projecting the path of the oncoming pack, Balulu marked a red-tinted boulder in the gully.

Quickly he shifted his eyes to a rock directly before him, and in his mind's eye imagined a she thylacine trailed by her cub. Their combined length equaled the distance between the rock and himself. For a second Balulu closed his eyes, and while they were shut he conjured up a mental image of a long line of she thylacines followed by cubs. Traveling single file, the line began at the reddish boulder on the gully's floor and extended up the slope to where he stood. When he opened his eyes, Balulu knew the distance from his stand to the red boulder.

In his mind's eye, Balulu threw his boomerang. He threw again, and again, using the second and third throws to compensate for errors in the first. When a thylacine appeared a few jumps behind the reddish boulder, translating mental practice into action was almost reflex. Balulu threw his boomerang. He watched it spin into the air, arc downward, and meet squarely the thylacine that was running just to the left of the reddish boulder.

Now there were only two thylacines left, but even though both had left the concealing scrub, Balulu had no more boomerangs.

Having thrown two, for perfect hits, the feel of a boomerang remained in his hand and his mind was adjusted to that weapon. It was difficult now to change over to a spear and impossible to use it

with the same precise timing. He must still do his
best, for a spear represented his only remaining
hope of killing still a third tiger before the remaining two came to grips with him.

Balulu fitted a spear in his *womera* and poised
for throwing. He glanced down the slope at the
two onrushing thylacines, and as a matter of common sense chose the nearer. But there was no
time left to estimate range or to throw a few im-
aginary spears for practice. He must use all the
skill he had, and hope for the best.

He threw the first spear. It swished from the
womera like some hissing, deadly viper and sang
onward. For a moment it seemed perfectly on
target. Then it struck just to the side of the thylacine, and a little dust cloud exploded where the
point imbedded itself.

Balulu snatched up his second spear. He did
not fit it into the *womera* for the thylacines were
so close now that he could cast with his arm
alone. But if he should miss with his remaining
spear he would have to face both beasts with
nothing but his stabbing stick, whose handle was

too short to deal with the raking claws and snapping fangs of a marsupial tiger.

On sudden impulse he knelt, thrusting the long spear before him as though it were a lance and bracing its butt against his own horny foot. He was aware of Warrigal flashing forward to engage one of the two thylacines, and heard the dingo's growls mingle with the tiger's hoarse snarls. Then he had time only for the thylacine that was rushing him.

As the creature sprang, he shifted and sighted his spear accordingly. The thylacine leaped and for a moment seemed to linger in the air. Then it came down on the spear with a thudding jar that threatened to throw Balulu off balance. He braced himself and felt the stone point bite into flesh.

Suddenly the spear shaft shattered in Balulu's hands.

Throwing himself backward, Balulu snatched up his stabbing stick and rushed the wounded thylacine, which was madly clawing at the spearhead embedded in its chest. Thrusting down with all his strength, Balulu caught the beast just behind the shoulder. The sharp flint head sank from sight. Twisting the shaft, Balulu wrenched out the stabbing stick and thrust again. The thylacine jerked convulsively, then went limp.

Balulu pulled his stabbing stick from the dead tiger and looked about for Warrigal.

He saw his brother ten yards away, locked in furious battle with the remaining thylacine, and both so covered with blood that it was impossible to tell which was more wounded. Balulu rushed to the pair and poised nearby with his stabbing stick raised. Warrigal and his enemy were struggling so fiercely and changing places so quickly that it was impossible to strike. He might kill the dingo.

Then, for a fleeting second, the thylacine's stripes were clearly exposed and Balulu thrust. The flint head bit deeply, and the fight was over.

Warrigal rolled away from the dead beast and limped to Balulu, who looked down at the big dingo proudly.

"Brother," he said, "we have killed all four. We are mighty hunters."

It was true. In normal times their feat would have brought them the highest of honors and become part of the legend of the Desert People. Many hunters had been routed by a single thylacine. Few had killed even one, let alone four in a single encounter.

But now, Balulu reflected glumly, his tribesmen thought only of their bellies. When he laid the dead thylacines at Loorola's sacred rock, it would be the meat they would be interested in, not the manner of its getting. And how was he to carry four beasts back to camp, for that matter?

He glanced into the gully only to see three of the five dingoes that had been following make off with the thylacine that lay beside the red-hued boulder. Up on the opposite slope, the two remaining dingoes were dragging the first tiger through the scrub. The wild dingoes, his brothers, knew hunger too, Balulu reflected. Perhaps, when the time came to grant a favor, they would remember whence came the meat upon which they now fed. Or perhaps they owed him no favor, since they had already granted one. With both boomerangs thrown, one spear cast and the other shattered, Balulu had only his stabbing stick. So armed, he might well have been attacked and killed by the wild dingoes, had they not been diverted by the two dead thylacines.

Balulu shouldered the dead tiger with which Warrigal had been fighting and carried it to where its pack mate lay. On the way he made a wide circle around his shattered spear. It had proved false, and to touch it or even go too near might invoke the displeasure of whatever devil had caused it to shatter. The other spear he must have. Balulu worked down the slope until he found and retrieved it.

When a throwing spear was again in his hands, he felt a rebirth of confidence that the stabbing stick alone could not give him. His confidence increased when he recovered the boomerang lying near the reddish boulder, and mounted again when he found his second boomerang. Off in the scrub, he could hear the wild dingoes snapping and snarling as they fought over the remains of the thylacines they had dragged away.

Warrigal at his heels and weapons in hand, Balulu retraced his steps to the top of the slope where he had left the bodies of the two tigers. Retrieving the rest of his equipment, he shouldered one of the thylacines. Then, equipment in one hand and with the other dragging the second tiger by the hind legs, he started back to camp.

It was almost dark when he reached the swale where the tribe was encamped. He went straight to the sacred boulder and deposited the two thylacines. Cutting a portion from one with the sharp flint head of his stabbing stick, he headed for his own sleeping spot, ignoring the tribesmen who were now clustering around the thylacines. Balulu fed Warrigal, built up his fire, cooked and ate a large piece of tiger meat, and was asleep almost as soon as he had eaten the last mouthful.

The next morning Balulu was up at the first faint signs of day. He and Warrigal ate what was left of their meat, left the swale, and drank their fill at the water hole. Then they headed directly away from the tribe at its camp. An hour later, on top of a desolate hill, they looked down into a shallow depression. Scarcely thirty feet from rim to rim, it was littered with stones that ranged from pebbles to rocks the size of a man's clenched fist. Nowhere else in the desert did Balulu know where such stones were to be found.

Walking among them, Balulu stooped to gather up one after another. He examined each minutely. Stone after stone was picked up and studied before he found three that passed his critical inspection.

The stones carefully stored in the pouch he wore hung about his neck, Balulu quartered away in a different direction and maintained a steady trot, Warrigal panting patiently at his heels. Two hours before dark, he came to a great, moon-shaped crater half filled with dead, sapling-sized trees from which the life had long since departed. But over the years, in the dry desert air, the little trees had not only not rotted, but had grown in resilient strength.

Balulu chose one and twisted it loose from its

roots. He hacked the springy twigs away with the head of his stabbing stick, then carried the trunk to a pile of boulders and wedged one end in a cleft. Placing one foot upon the unsupported trunk, he shoved sharply downward. The slender trunk did not break. Balulu placed his second foot beside his first, and let the trunk bear his whole weight. It did not break until he leaped up and down on it.

The next one broke, and the next, but the fourth yielded to no strain he could devise. Satisfied at last, Balulu gathered wood for a fire. He kindled it by heaping flimsy tinder about one of the fire sticks, inserting the point of the other in a slot in the first, and spinning the upright stick between his palms. As friction built up, the tinder smoked, glowed, then ignited. Balulu fed his fire, then, as darkness gathered, collected a pile of wood large enough to last through the night. By the time it was too dark to see, he and Warrigal were both asleep.

The next morning Balulu went to work on his new spear. The shaft he had finally chosen was already almost the correct diameter and perfectly straight. But with absorbed concentration Balulu used the sharp edge of one of his stones to smooth knots where the twigs had joined the trunk and to remove all other imperfections. Then, scraping a single thin shaving at a time, he used the same stone to make his stick an even circumference its whole length. Finally he tested for balance by laying the stick on an upthrust finger and whirling it. Not satisfied, he resumed scraping.

When he finally approved of the shaft, he began working his stones. Using one stone to strike the other, he chipped away a flake at a time. It was slow, laborious work, but he finally inserted the pointed spearhead that had been a stone into a cleft at one end of a spear haft that had been a seasoned sapling.

Balulu bound head to haft with thin strips of gut from one of the dead thylacines, then built up his fire and held the spearhead close to the flames. Contracting and tightening as it dried, the gut also turned iron-hard. When Balulu was finished, it was impossible to wrench head from haft.

Balulu balanced his new spear in his hand and found it good. He chose a mark some distance away, a small clump of spinifex grass. Resting the spear in his *womera*, Balulu cast. The stone point sliced cleanly through the clump of spinifex and the shaft quivered rhythmically as the point buried itself in the earth.

Retrieving his new spear, Balulu added it to his other weapons and started toward camp. His e-quipment was once more complete.

CHAPTER FOUR

The Council of Elders was gathered in solemn conclave. Cross-legged, they sat in a rough circle around the sacred Rock of the Four Winds. Loorola, the Witch Doctor, was dancing around the rock, making appropriate magic. His naked body was adorned with white stripes for good spirits and black stripes for bad ones. The white stripes were noticeably thin and feeble, the black ones were wide and bold.

The circle symbolized the horizon, the elders represented the dominating force and ruling body of the Desert People. Rono, as was proper, occupied the chief's honored position at the rock's

northernmost tip. The others were seated as befitted their station, with the most distinguished
nearest Rono.

Not entitled to a voice in the Council, but sitting near enough to overhear, were Balulu and
the other young men. Beyond them were the boys,
and still farther away, beyond earshot, the wom-
en and girls were gathered.

In any normal circumstances, Loorola would
have been foremost in influencing the policy-
making body. But because of his proved inability
to banish the Devil Who Lived Where the River
Had Flowed, the Witch Doctor had lost much of
the tribe's faith and confidence. Only Rono retained any real authority in the council.

Balulu turned his eyes from Loorola's magic-
making to look out over the camp. At the far end
sat a wizened figure, old Mooeeanga, with his
back against a sun-warmed boulder. Balulu knew
that he was gazing at visions which appeared to
his eyes only. Even before the Devil dried all the
water and caused the present famine, old Mooeeanga had gone to dwell in that unreal world

known only to the very old and the very young.

Balulu saw a woman come up from the dry and pebble-littered river bed. On her head she balanced a hollowed-out wooden carrying dish. In her hand was a yard-long digging stick whose point had first been charred to make it hard and then sharpened so it would pierce the earth. All women of the tribe used such sticks to dig edible roots and such dishes to carry them, and in former good times no woman went root hunting without filling her dish. Balulu was sure that this dish was empty, for there was nothing edible left to dig in the dry river bed.

The woman walked directly to a fire near where old Mooeeanga entranced himself with visions. The woman squatted beside a young child who was lying back against a boulder as though asleep. The woman looked around, then her hand brushed the child's mouth and at once moved away. The child sat suddenly upright and began to move its jaws. It was eating something!

Balulu felt a glow of satisfaction. As conditions had grown worse, he had observed uneasily that the gap between humans and beasts drew ever more narrow. But that was not the case here. The woman had not only not eaten the food where she had found it, as she might well have done, but she had defied Rono, sure punishment for breaking the rule of common sharing, and even her own hunger, so that her child might eat. It was a happy thing to see.

Rono began to speak and Balulu turned back to the Council of Elders.

"We have made many camps," Rono was saying, "and we have journeyed beneath many suns. We have visited all places where once we found game in plenty, and even at the best of them we found only enough food to keep the spark of life glowing. Many of the old and weak are already dead."

There was a wailing murmur of assent from the listening elders. Loorola pointed his face to the sky and moved his right leg and left arm in symbolic gestures. The elders watched him with hopeless indifference.

"We are not dead," Rono went on, "but not for

long shall we live without food. No hunter has brought in game while the last two suns rose and set. I have thought much about this. I have found a way to bring game to us."

At this statement, an exclamation of amazement went around the circle, then subsided to respectful attention. Rono gestured toward the scrub.

"The wild dingoes still follow us," he announced, "even as they have followed us since it became clear that there is no food elsewhere. Now and again they have killed and eaten one of us, but it is equally true that now and again we have killed and eaten a dingo. We have not been able to kill more, for always they run away from us. But we will kill many if we bring them near, and I have found a way."

The council sat in breathless silence. Even Loorola forgot to finger his charms and undulate his body. Rono waited a moment.

"A hungry dingo is not a senseless dingo," he said finally. "When we come with weapons they run away because they know we will kill them if they do not. But a famished dingo with meat before it takes leave of its senses. Nothing can make it run away, not even a spear in the ribs. We shall give the dingoes food. While they are busy eating, we shall kill as many as we please."

Rono pointed at the wizened figure sitting by itself.

"Except in the body, Mooeeanga has not been among us for many seasons. Nor is he of use in the hunt, or in war, or in anything save staring at strange visions known to him alone. He has already left us in mind; let him leave us in body, for the good of the tribe. We will take him out in the scrub, and return here. The wild dingoes will not attack him at once because they will know even Mooeeanga is a man. But they will not hesitate as soon as they are sure he is a helpless man. While the dingoes are busy devouring Mooeeanga, we shall approach with our weapons and make a great killing."

Balulu waited expectantly for shouts of outraged indignation to answer a proposal so outrageous. There was nothing save silence, that presently gave way to subdued murmurs as the elders exchanged opinions. Balulu turned his eyes away. Devils lived not only in the river, but also in the thoughts of his fellow tribesmen.

An elder named Tarm made himself heard. "It is true that Mooeeanga is very old," he stated. "It is equally true that he is no longer with us."

An older man, a member of the Emu Totem said angrily, "Mooeeanga's age does indeed render him useless. But he did his share, and more, before most of us even learned to handle a spear. He brought more meat to this tribe than any other hunter."

"Then it is right that Mooeeanga again supply food in this time of desperate need," Rono replied. "Does anyone doubt that Rono speaks truly? If we have no food soon, there will be none left to eat what may come too late."

"I think Mooeeanga would never know what happened," said an elder who wore the esteemed emu plume. "His thoughts are ever far away from what happens here."

Sick at heart, nevertheless Balulu was fully aware that no single member of the council was solely responsible for the final dreadful verdict. Perhaps even most wished to oppose the decision. But the devil now gnawing at their bellies was so powerful that it could steal from a man all that made him a man. Furthermore, Balulu knew, each elder in the council thought that he was merely carrying out the wishes of every other man.

As the council broke up, and advanced in a body on the old man, Balulu could only look on helplessly.

When the men who had taken old Mooeeanga out into the scrub returned to camp, Balulu watched them come back. That portion of his hunter's brain which noted and analyzed everything told him that they had gone farther from camp than they should, if their dreadful plan was to work. He, Balulu, was of the Dingo Totem and understood the ways of his wild brothers.

As though in verification, before the returning elders had reached their own fires the air was split by a thin scream that was instantly lost in a bedlam of growls and snarls. Weapons in hand, the aborigines raced back in the direction from which they had just come.

This time Balulu did not turn to watch, for he already knew the outcome. The hunters were too late. By the time they arrived, the wild dingoes would have torn Mooeeanga to pieces and disappeared in the bush again.

He was right, for presently the hunters came straggling back, empty handed. Rono, in the lead, made straight for Balulu.

Balulu rose. Warrigal beside him, he faced the angry leader.

"You are of the Dingo Totem," Rono declared, "and know the ways of your wild brothers. You knew we would fail."

Balulu said nothing.

"Tomorrow," Rono continued, "we shall try another bait, but before we may hope for success we must eat the flesh of a dingo. Do you hear?"

"I hear," said Balulu.

Saying nothing else, Balulu turned and walked away. He passed the woman who had flouted tribal law and defied death itself so that her child might have a morsel of food, but he did not look into her face. Instead, he looked at the child, now asleep.

The problem he faced was almost as simple and fundamental as the woman's. The tribe was starving. If it did not eat, it would perish. If the death of Warrigal would prevent starvation, then his death meant nothing. But at best it would only postpone starvation. It was not the answer. Unless a constant source of food was provided, many more, perhaps all the tribe, would die.

Before the drought, the Desert People had been happy and well fed. Then came the Devil Who Lived Where the River Had Flowed, and at first Balulu had accepted without question the thought that an evil spirit was indeed responsible for all their misery. But that had come about almost three years ago, and Balulu had missed no opportunity to watch the river. He had yet to see a single sign of any devil. Nor, except for Loorola, would anyone else admit seeing one. Long ago, Balulu had formed serious doubts that any evil spirit existed in the river.

If there was no devil, then the entire tribe lived in fear of something which did not even exist. Was this devil an excuse for avoiding responsibility for their fate? In any event, if the tribe stayed here and no rain came, it would eventually starve, devil or no devil. If water and game existed elsewhere, someone must find it out and lead the tribe there before it was too late. If he, Balulu met death while searching, what besides death did he face if he failed to search?

When night fell, Balulu tied his belt about his middle and hung his pouch around his neck. Boomerangs in one hand, spears and fire sticks in the other, and Warrigal trailing, he stole away as quietly as a shadow. He stopped at the water hole only long enough for Warrigal and himself to drink their fill, then started off through the night at a fast trot.

A few moments after leaving the water hole, his keen senses told him that the wild dingoes had already fallen in on his trail.

CHAPTER FIVE

Warrigal brushed his thigh with a cold nose and Balulu found a sudden reassurance in the act. He was not alone, his brother was telling him. Balulu had saved Warrigal from the cooking fires and Warrigal would not forget.

Actually, Rono's order had merely set in motion a plan Balulu had been considering anyway. The conviction had been growing in him that if there was so very little hope here on the desert, there could scarcely be less elsewhere. He who went to find out risked only the death he was already facing. At the same time he could have hope of finding a new supply of game somewhere, not for himself alone but for the tribe too.

Stars sprinkled across a clear night sky cast a wan glow that revealed portions of the parched desert landscape in faint relief but made the shadows even blacker. Since the feeble light was little aid to seeing, Balulu did not rely on his eyes, nor did he need to.

Thoroughly familiar with every inch of this terrain, he guided himself partly by instinct and partly by the way the earth felt to the soles of his bare feet. The course he had set would take him back through the Desert People's former hunting grounds in the mountains. He knew perfectly well that the drought also prevailed there, and that life in the uplands was even more uncertain than on the desert. But what lay beyond the farthest known point in the tablelands? If the wild dingoes would spare him and if he did not die of thirst, he would find out.

Balulu had been detected and was presently being followed by four dingoes: a grizzled old dog, his mate, and two half-grown cubs that still survived from this pair's last litter. The old dog, undisputed leader of the group, conducted himself as befitted a hunter of experience and wisdom. With quarry in prospect he was eager, but even hunger could not make him forsake caution.

The old dog knew exactly what he was doing. Veteran of numerous skirmishes with men, he had been the one to lead the attack on the helpless Mooeeanga. But he had sensed that Mooeeanga was helpless. Balulu was not; experience told the old dog that a man and a tame dingo traveling together were always dangerous. The limp in one leg, caused by an old spear wound, never let him forget the fact. He knew the power of men, and did not intend to be hurt again. Although he would not hesitate to attack the man and the tame dingo if circumstances seemed right, he preferred to follow in hopes of sharing any kill the man might make.

Emboldened when no weapons came their way, the younger dingoes moved up to close the gap between themselves and Balulu, then slowed to adjust their pace to his. The older dingoes held back, for they knew that the younger ones were now within range of the man's weapons.

Balulu knew it too, and speculated on this new development as he maintained his steady trot toward the mountains. Even though he could not outrun the wild dingoes, he did not greatly fear them. He knew what they intended. The only real danger, at least for the moment, lay in the possibility that the two over-anxious dingoes that had moved nearer might try to rush him.

Though he could not see the young dingoes, Balulu knew where they were. In the darkness neither spear nor boomerang could be used with accuracy, but there was still a chance of hitting one of them. Balulu decided against trying. With a limited store of weapons, he couldn't afford to throw any that couldn't be recovered. Furthermore, he was of the Dingo Totem, and what grim consequences might have to be faced if he killed a wild brother? That, however, must not stop him. He had set out to find food for the tribe, and any personal misfortune he might suffer while so doing must be incidental.

Balulu comforted himself with the fact that the wild dingoes on his trail were his brothers who owed him the same allegiance he owed them. But they were beasts, not men, and might kill and eat him, because they were beasts. Balulu was a man. Therefore he must kill dingoes only if there was no other way to carry on his mission.

He made his plans as he trotted on. First he must elude the wild dingoes. After that he must deal with the vengeful Rono, who would spare no effort to capture and punish one so openly defiant of his orders. Balulu hoped to achieve both objectives with the same maneuver.

A few miles to the east were some rocky escarpments that a man could climb but a dingo could not. That posed no problem as far as Warrigal was concerned, for Balulu would lift him from ledge to ledge. On top of the escarpments was a desolate tableland where hunting had been poor even in the best of times. Few hunters had ever found it worth their while to visit such a forbidding place.

It was scarcely an inviting prospect, but it

seemed to be the only feasible course. The dingoes could not climb the escarpment, and since
there was no game on the tableland, there was
little prospect of running across wild dingoes that
might have ascended by other paths. By the same
token, once Balulu was on the tableland, the most
zealous among the pursuing hunters would find
his enthusiasm flagging at thought of entering
such a place.

How he would survive when, and if, he gained
such a barren haven was a matter Balulu could
only consider when the time came. For the present he would concentrate on reaching the tableland.

When three more wild dingoes quartered out
of the darkness to fall in with the pack on Balulu's
trail, they were instantly resented by the four already there. The newcomers were two-year-old
males, keeping each other's company only because as yet they had not found mates. They were
strangers to the grizzled old dog dingo, and as

such, unwelcome. Furthermore, the dingoes who had come first regarded the quarry they were following as their personal property.

The old male snarled, a fierce and throaty sound that was not a warning but an outright demand that his priority rights be respected. The result was a short, sharp exchange of snarls, growls and snapping teeth as the old male gave the leader of the trio a practical lesson on exactly what he meant. A shrill yelp of pain announced the newcomer's submission to authority, at least temporarily.

A hope that flared in Balulu when he heard the fight start faded as soon as the snarls stopped. Though he was pledged not to kill dingoes, in no way would he be responsible if they killed each other. Should even one go down, the rest would stop long enough to tear apart and eat the fallen pack mate.

Now that the dingo pack was larger, it was getting bolder. Balulu knew that he could hope to reach the rocky escarpments only if he could somehow gain time, and he could gain time only if something frightened or delayed the pack. But what?

As Balulu trotted on, he saw before him the dim outline of a ledge of stone he knew. He and Warrigal would have to make a stand there, where the ledge would offer protection for their backs. Only a little way beyond the ledge, but a hopeless distance unless the pack was delayed, were the stone escarpments leading to the bleak tableland.

As Balulu approached the ledge, he suddenly smelled a sickishly sweet, faint odor. The leaders of the pack were all but snapping at his heels when Balulu jumped in the air and raced on past the ledge.

Behind him, he heard first a shrill yelp, then a medley of frightened snarls and growls. Because he had not had to be false to his totem, Balulu breathed quick, silent thanks and ran on. He had smelled the deadly black snake in time and jumped clear over it. Straining to the kill, oblivious to everything else, the dingoes had blundered onto the aroused snake.

Balulu reached the escarpment and scrambled up a few feet. Turning, he searched the darkness beneath him. Where was Warrigal?

But his brother was no longer with him. Balulu listened, but could hear nothing at all except the wild pack, now reassembled and again in pursuit. The dingoes reached the foot of the escarpment and leaped again and again, trying to pull Balulu down.

Alone, and with a heavy heart, Balulu crouched on a narrow ledge.

CHAPTER SIX

The rising sun painted a golden fan across the horizon, then presently a slanting beam fell across the desolate tableland. The sun seemed to falter, as if hesitant to illumine a place so dead. The sun could bring warmth, but no cheer to such a place.

The tableland consisted of strips of baked red earth separated by belts of dun gray rock. No trees had ever grown here, and the only sign that life had ever existed were low, shrub-like skeletons, the brittle bones of near-indestructible plants that had needed ages just to learn how to survive in such desolation.

The first sunbeam awakened Balulu. Numb

with cold, he rose from the spot where he had
fallen when he finally reached the summit last
night and moved to the sunny side of a boulder.
He peered into the lowland from which he had
come and which still lay in semi-gloom, for the
sun had not yet reached there.

What had happened to Warrigal? There were
only two possible explanations for his absence.
The dingo had either been killed by the wild pack
or else had fled by himself after the encounter
with the snake. He had not reached the escarpment, for Balulu had continued to linger until he
had grown cold and stiff, and feared he would
fall. He had begun to climb, inching his way up,
for the ascent, difficult enough by day, was infinitely more so at night. When he had finally
reached the top he was too exhausted to do anything save throw himself down and sleep. He
hadn't even thought of a fire, sure that nothing
was alive on the crest but himself.

Now he must go on. The journey would be far
longer and harder without his brother but he must
go. Balulu inspected his weapons and started.

Not again did he look back. As the chill of the night gave away to the heat of the day, he struck a moderate pace, for there was a very great distance to go. He noted the dead earth with its dead vegetation but was neither discouraged nor afraid. He had known what he would find here before he left camp.

The distance did not daunt Balulu, for his people were born to wander. In addition he was blessed with an asset almost equal to his weapons. He was capable of living completely for the moment, the moment that was here to be faced, and never mind the next moment until he must face that one. Only by making fullest use of the time at hand did he expect success in long-range plans.

After three hours, he sat down on the shady side of a boulder and rested his head on drawn-up knees. Lofty mountains beckoned in the haze-shrouded distance, but Balulu did not worry because he could do nothing about them unless and until he got there. Three full hours had scarcely put him well onto the bleak tableland, and he would do first things first.

His alert senses, keen as any wild thing's, were aware of everything about him. He smelled the parched earth and heard the rattle of the skeleton scrub. He felt the sun, the hot wind, and the earth on his bare feet. And as soon as he stopped to rest, he began to feel thirst.

That was neither surprising nor frightening, for he had known there was no water here. If he did not find some, in time he would be unable to go on. But for the present his thirst was merely an awareness, not a need. Rested, Balulu rose and continued toward the mountains.

The sun was still well above the horizon when a faint chill warned that a hot day was about to end and a cold night to begin. Balulu began to think about a favorable camp. Ordinarily, since he was traveling alone, his choice would have fallen on some spot that promised shelter from the wind and at the same time could be easily defended. Here in this land of no life the only enemies were heat and cold, hunger and thirst. Since none of them could be fought with weapons, there was no need to think of defense.

Balulu went on at the same moderate pace. He might have traveled faster, and if there had been any assurance of finding strength-sustaining food and water, he would have put many more miles behind. As things were, if he ran at top speed all day he would only increase his thirst to the point where he would end his journey before he had really begun it. By sparing himself he could go farther.

An hour of daylight still remained when Balulu stopped beside a straight-sided boulder that stood only a few feet from another. The cold was increasing as the sun declined, and Balulu decided to make camp before he became chilled through.

He gathered dead twigs and branches from the lifeless scrub and carried them to his rock. When he had a pile of wood large enough to suit him, he took his fire sticks and a bit of tinder from his pouch, and lighted a fire between the two boulders. Then he sat with his back against the large boulder and his head resting on upraised knees. The brittle wood burned fast, but the first leaping blaze began to warm the straight side of the large boulder. All night it could be kept warm, and the fire made to reflect a comfortable heat between the two boulders simply by adding a stick or two when the embers burned low.

Balulu fell into a doze that was presently disturbed by a troublesome dream. The dream took him back to the water hole where the tribe was camped. He was very thirsty, but just as he threw himself beside the water hole, all the water disappeared in the ground, leaving only dried mud. He awoke trembling and found his tongue licking parched lips. For a few minutes he stared nervously at the tiny fire, afraid to go back to sleep. He told himself that he was far from that water hole anyway, and did his best to force the picture from his mind. It was a bad sign for a thirsty man to dream of water. Not for a long while would he let himself go back to sleep. Finally he did, his last waking thought a determination that if he would be visited by dreams, they must not be dreams of water.

This time another dream came. He was making his way across the arid tableland when, to his boundless astonishment, he saw a dingo. It was a young, sleek, and full-furred adult that looked exactly like Warrigal. Knowing it could not be Warrigal, Balulu expected an attack and was raising his boomerang when the dingo spoke.

"Do not throw your boomerang, Balulu," the dingo said. "I am the spirit of the Dingo Totem. I am your brother, Warrigal."

Lowering his boomerang, Balulu looked more closely and saw that this was indeed Warrigal.

"I have found you again, Warrigal," Balulu said happily. "It is a glad meeting."

Warrigal answered, "We were fated to meet so we might travel side by side again. Shall we go on?"

"Let us go on," said Balulu.

"Follow me, brother."

Warrigal led the way and Balulu fell in behind. Until now he had not been at all sure of his fate in this dead land, but now he was certain all would be well. Warrigal would lead him to safety.

The dingo vanished like a raindrop in the dust and Balulu awoke to stare at his dying fire. He added a couple of sticks and watched flame rise about them, but the vision of Warrigal remained in his mind. Somehow it seemed not a dream at all, but reality. The confidence that had come upon Balulu while he slept remained with him.

Almost at once he returned to sleep, and this time slept until the rising sun roused him to a new day and a new disappointment. Again the night had been cold, but not cold enough to leave a rime of frost on the boulders that he could lick off. Nor was there any dew to slake his thirst.

Balulu made his daily inspection of weapons and continued toward the mountains. He started at the same pace he had kept the previous day, but though he wondered if he could continue all day without water, he was not as troubled as he had been. Last night's vision of Warrigal did not vanish with the sun. Sustained by faith in his dreams, Balulu went on.

The sun was three hours high when he halted in his tracks. Some distance to one side, the barest flicker of motion told him that he had finally found another living thing in this place of no life.

It was a foot-long lizard that either had its own source of food and water or somehow managed to stay alive without either. After the betraying flick of its tail that Balulu had seen, it was lying quietly in the shade of a rock.

Balulu threw a boomerang, watched it fly true to its mark, and trotted over to retrieve his game and his boomerang. The skinny lizard was scarcely a morsel, he could eat a dozen such, but that was unimportant. What really mattered was that he had found food where he had expected none. Warrigal had indeed spoken truly in his dream; finding the lizard was surely a promise of that.

That night, sitting over his next fire, Balulu fell asleep with eager anticipation. Warrigal would come again with more good tidings and wise counsel. But throughout the night the spirit of the Dingo Totem did not come.

The morning sun brought doubt and anxiety. Why had Warrigal brought hope and then deserted him? Balulu thought uneasily of the black snake, and of how he had lured the dingo pack to it. Was this his punishment?

Balulu did not know where he was, or how
many night fires were behind him, or anything
else except that he lay panting beneath a burning
sun, when he heard and recognized a voice.

"Get up, brother," said Warrigal. "You will die
if you do not."

Balulu stirred feebly. In his spinning head were
vague memories of mounting thirst that had become unendurable, and of a body that would no
longer obey his will. He had fallen, he recalled,
and he had not been able to get up. He did not
want to get up, but now it seemed that he must.
Balulu opened his eyes.

A few feet away was Warrigal, watching him
steadily. Balulu smiled.

"Come," Warrigal said. "Follow me."

Balulu tried to answer, but no sound came from
his parched and swollen lips. Clawing desperately
with both hands and pushing with his feet, Balulu
crawled part way up the face of a boulder, rested,
made a supreme effort, and gained his feet.

Warrigal was still watching, and when Balulu

lurched forward, the dingo moved backward. Supporting himself with his stabbing stick, Balulu staggered on. The sun seemed to dim and the day darken, but it was not the darkness of full night. Balulu tottered after Warrigal, pushed through a bed of shriveled reeds, and fell prone on a patch of sun-dried mud.

Raising himself on his elbows, he began to dig with his stabbing stick.

CHAPTER SEVEN

When Balulu secretly stole away from the camp of the Desert People, Warrigal had fallen in beside him as a matter of course. Even though they were leaving at night, which was both unusual and dangerous, the dingo had no thought of staying behind in camp.

Although Warrigal had been born wild, he had been captured and tamed as a young puppy, and so had never run with the wild packs. His knowledge of pack life was limited to those instincts and yearnings which can never be completely lost by any member of the dog family, even the most pampered of pets. But his hunting skill was equal to that of any wild dingo and had been further sharpened by hunting with Balulu. Warrigal had learned much that no wild dingo ever learns. His natural intelligence and ability to grasp different situations had responded readily to Balulu's teaching. Over the years Warrigal had not only learned to hunt as Balulu had taught him, but even improved on some of his teacher's methods. He knew that the object of hunting was not merely to find game, but to maneuver in such a fashion that anything they found would come or could be driven into a position that would enable Balulu to bring it down. Their hunts followed no routine pattern but each instance must be shaped by the circumstances attending it. Their leaving the tribe's camp at night was, to Warrigal, merely new circumstances.

As they left the fires behind, Warrigal was fully aware of the wild dingoes lurking nearby and of the danger they represented. But they did not worry him. Not only were they his own kind, but he and Balulu had faced danger so many times that it had come to be a normal way of life.

He knew at once when the first pack of wild dingoes, the grizzled old dog and his family, took up the trail and his analysis of them was even more penetrating than Balulu's. He knew that they had every intention of attacking, but not until a favorable opportunity presented.

Though his nerves were taut and his reflexes keyed to the utmost, Warrigal was not afraid. Dingoes often fought with others of their kind, sometimes to the death. But Warrigal considered himself a match for any wild representatives of his kind. He instinctively knew that he had little to fear unless he was hurt so seriously that he could not defend himself. Wild dingoes tolerated tame ones, and did not regard them as outcasts or enemies simply because they hunted and lived with men. Warrigal was more concerned over Balulu's safety than his own.

He knew when the three young males joined the family of four, and understood the greatly increased danger brought about by the changed situation. But aside from falling a few steps behind Balulu, he did nothing. There was nothing to do until the pack closed in, no possibility of planning in advance because there was no way of knowing what form the attack might take.

As Balulu approached the stone ledge where he planned to make a stand, Warrigal sensed a change of attitude in the pack behind them; it was closing in. Never one to wait until a fight was carried to him, Warrigal chose to take the offensive now. He dropped back and grappled with a lean young male that was running neck and neck with the grizzled leader. Momentarily disconcerted by this unexpected interruption, the others slowed their rush. Though neither Warrigal nor Balulu were aware of it, that fleeting pause brought the black snake's odor to Balulu, gave him time to change course, leap over the snake, and run on. When the pack raced on, Warrigal broke away from his enemy and tried to run on so that he might be nearer Balulu. But the other dingo would have none of it. He had not started the fight, but he was more than willing to finish it. He lunged, striking the tame dingo with his shoulder and hoping to send him sprawling.

But Warrigal was no stranger to rough and tumble fighting. He sidestepped as his enemy lunged, then jackknifed his body to clash at the other's flank. Cowed by such a fierce attack, the other dingo retreated. Warrigal followed, crowding his foe and slashing as he advanced. The wild dingo made another stand and for a time fought savagely. Then he whirled and ran.

Hot with battle lust, thinking only of the kill, Warrigal streaked across the desert after his fleeing enemy. He was miles away when, for the first time since starting the fight, he remembered Balulu. Warrigal stopped in mid leap, swapped ends, and raced back to where he had left the aborigine.

He read the story of what had taken place by the scents left behind, then singled out Balulu's trail and followed it to the base of the escarpment. There he raised his head to peer upward, letting his nose tell him that the man had gone where a dingo could not hope to follow. He reared against the smooth rock, whining anxiously as he sought a ledge or other foothold. There was none.

Quickly taking in the situation, Warrigal did

not whine and fuss, as a tame dog might have, or
waste time looking at the escarpment in a vain
hope that he would find a way up if he looked
long enough. Warrigal knew only that Balulu had
seen fit to climb up to the tableland and that he
must contrive to get there too if he hoped to rejoin him. Since he could not scale the escarpment
at this spot, obviously he must find another way.
Warrigal swung westward, following the base of
the sheer cliff in search of a path up.

Actually the escarpments were only one seg-
ment of an unbroken wall, the face of which had
been so relentlessly scoured by sand and wind
that it presented nothing but a smooth and almost
perpendicular surface. It fenced in much of the
bleak tableland, and extended for so many miles
that night had changed to day and day had become high noon before Warrigal found a break he
could climb. Without the faintest hesitation, the
dingo went up.

Once on top, he began to run at full speed, for
the faster he traveled the sooner he would find
Balulu. Finally he came to a bewildered halt.

The bleak, flat upland was strange country. Not only had he never before visited it, but he'd never seen anything similar. The winds on the summit were gusty and fitful, interlaced with cross currents that made orientation a virtual impossibility. When he started out he was positive that the course he chose led straight to the escarpments, and once there he'd have no trouble picking up Balulu's trail. But he was in error.

Baffled, Warrigal was not discouraged. All he knew was that Balulu had climbed up to this tableland. The dingo would either find him or find that he had gone elsewhere. If the latter, he would continue to search.

Warrigal approached the problem his own way. There was little point in quartering methodically back and forth when, by scaling some eminence where the winds converged, his nose could tell him all he wanted to know anyway. He traveled as no human would have thought of searching, sometimes casting about with almost painful thoroughness and sometimes ignoring entirely a large area that a human would have explored. But when Warrigal went on, he knew all he needed to about what lay behind him.

Even as he worked as a dingo, so he lived as one. Though his nose was not too much keener than Balulu's and his eyes greatly inferior, his marvelous ears heard tiny sounds that no human could ever detect. Often he caught and ate small snakes whose presence Balulu never suspected because, though they carried almost no scent, Warrigal heard them wriggling in their hidden crevices and dug them out. Once he feasted on fat grasshoppers which, blown by the wind, descended in a veritable swarm on the tableland.

Lack of water was tormenting but not unendurable. Occasionally his nose would lead him to moist smears in the shade of overhanging ledges, where he scraped and dug until a muddy seepage appeared, and lapped it up. It did not satisfy thirst, but it relieved the sharpest torments.

On the eighth day he found the bed of the dry lake.

Warrigal knew at once what it was and what it offered. The sun-baked surface, seamed and cracked, had once been the bottom of a large pond. Sniffing at the cracks, the dingo was searching for the best place to dig when he became suddenly aware of the scent that he had sought for so long.

His head snapped erect and his tail began to wag furiously. Never once had he doubted he would find Balulu and now at last he had done so. Warrigal bounded forward to discover Balulu lying quiet and unmoving on the scorched ground. He stopped short of the fallen hunter, puzzled by actions so unusual. Then he trotted on and licked Balulu's face. When the young aborigine first moaned and then stirred, Warrigal did a crazy little dance with his front feet.

Now that they were finally united, he and Balulu must be on with the hunt. But first he wanted to pursue the enticing odor of moisture that he had detected in the bottom of the dry lake. He waited patiently for Balulu to rise, then walked backward toward the lake. Bit by bit, waiting when Balulu faltered, Warrigal led him onward.

CHAPTER EIGHT

Strength now filled Balulu's body as spring rain fills a dry stream bed.

He had had to dig down as far as he was able to reach with both arms fully extended, but there he had found still-moist earth and a frog nearly the size of his head, as he had expected he would. Filling its body with water before the lake went wholly dry, and then burrowing deeply into still-soft mud, the frog could live there almost indefinitely, until rains eventually filled the lake again. Water trapped beneath the frog's stretched skin had served to ease Balulu's thirst and the frog itself had satisfied his hunger.

Balulu looked at the hole and the heap of dirt beside it, then out across the sun-baked and sun-cracked expanse of dried mud that stretched before him. This lake, unknown to the Desert People, had contained water in the not-too-distant past, proving that there had been rain here far more recently than in the part of the desert where Balulu's tribe lived. The power of the Devil Who Lived Where the River Had Flowed, if it existed, was not as strong here, certainly not as strong as the protecting magic of the Dingo Totem.

It had been the power of the Dingo Totem that had led him here, Balulu thought gratefully. Warrigal, his brother, had come to him, just as he had appeared in the dream. The meaning of the vows he had taken and the strength and help given to him because he had violated none of them were driven home to Balulu as never before. His confidence soared, for he had seen proof of the strength of his totem, both in his dreams and in reality. Now he would not fail.

Suddenly he became aware that Warrigal was sniffing in the hole where Balulu had found the frog, and licking the damp mud at the bottom. Balulu was filled with shame.

"Forgive me, brother, because I thought first of my own needs," he said softly. "My great want of water left me neither eyes nor thought for anything else. Now you, too, shall eat and drink."

He moved a little ways from the hole already dug and started probing the crust with his stabbing stick. The great, drum-voiced frogs that rippled these small upland lakes when water flowed were myriad in number. Even though many might have died with the drying lake, Balulu knew that there would be no lack of those that had buried themselves in mud to wait until the lake filled with water once more.

Where his stick pierced the hardened mud most readily, indicating softer ground, Balulu started another hole. He dug up a second frog, then a third, which Warrigal gobbled instantly. As he began probing for another frog for himself, Balulu pondered.

He had already come a very long way, though perhaps it was a short distance compared with what he still must travel. He had suffered much from both hunger and thirst while crossing the bleak tableland, and of the two, thirst had been by far the harder to bear. If there had been some way to carry water with him, obviously he would not have been thirsty. But how to carry it?

Water was not a solid substance that one might hold in his hand or store in his pouch. To attempt to seize it was to have it slip through the fingers. It could find the tiniest hole or crevice and drain away while one watched. Confining water in anything except one's own belly was so difficult that Balulu had never even thought about the possibility before.

With suddenly rising excitement he recalled that, following heavy rains, puddles of water were often trapped in the hollows and depressions that marked the surface boulders. His excitement subsided almost as soon as it came. Regardless of how many of its dips and hollows contained water, how could one carry the boulder? Even a rock small enough to be lifted would be a great hindrance on any journey. It was more sensible to

take one's chances on finding water than to stag-
ger under such a load.

Yet the idea would not leave Balulu's mind. It
was a notion with exciting possibilities. A hunter
who could carry his own water would no longer
need to limit his range to a day's journey from
known water holes. He could travel as far as Balulu had come—and farther—without danger of
perishing from thirst. But try as he would, Balulu
could imagine no container that would hold an
adequate supply of water and yet weigh so little
that it would not be an impractical burden.

In any event, he and Warrigal would have to
stay near the lake, the only dependable source of
food and water he knew, until he was rested and
felt like going on. Warrigal padding beside him,
he returned to the edge of the lake to look for a
place to camp. He pushed through withered reeds
that had been tall and green, and a lush breeding
ground for hordes of insects upon which the great
frogs had fed. Now the dead stalks snapped off
beneath his feet and little dust clouds rose as he
stepped on them.

Though there seemed to be not the faintest possibility of encountering enemies either beast or human in this forsaken place, Balulu took no chances and chose his camp with care. Finding a yard-wide rock ledge with an almost sheer wall of rock behind it, he backed off to inspect the place from a distance. He liked it. Nothing could come down the ledge, the front approaches were defensible, and once the rock wall was heated a very small fire would keep it comfortably warm while he slept.

Balulu set about gathering wood for his night fire, a simple task in a land of dead trees and shrubs that needed only to be pushed over and carried or dragged to his camp. Some of the trees were hollow, their branches gone, their trunks mere stub-like shells still held erect by their dead roots. Balulu took only a few of these, trying to find instead solid trunks that would burn longer and throw out more heat.

His wood arranged and fire kindled, Balulu went back out on the lake bottom to dig more frogs. He carried two back to camp, both swollen with stored-up water. Although he was hungry, he was no longer thirsty, and had no immediate use for the water contained in the frogs. At any other time Balulu would have simply thrown the water away. But he had been thirsty too recently to regard water lightly now. To save it, he hit upon the happy expedient of planting his left heel in the dry mud, throwing his full weight on it, and turning slowly until he had scooped a shallow saucer. He patted it firm with the palms of his hands and stored his surplus water in it.

For a moment he stood over the little puddle and regarded it intently. Though the water was slowly seeping into the earth, his improvised basin would hold some of it for a while. While certainly not efficient, this was another way to store water. But the puddle suggested no feasible way to carry it.

Balulu turned thoughtfully back to his fire. He did not know how far he must yet travel and lacked the smallest notion of the difficulties that might beset his path. But he had no doubt that all troubles would be lessened if he might be certain of water. Suddenly he had a glow of inspiration.

The containers he must have were in his very hands! The great frogs filled themselves with water and lost none of it even after many months passed. Obviously their skins were watertight! Excitedly, Balulu slit both frogs across the rear legs and peeled their skins off.

At once it became obvious that some mending was in order. Though he had made only one incision in each skin, holes gaped where the eyes, the nostrils, and the mouths had been. Considering a way to close them, Balulu hit upon the method of puckering the ends together and tying them with strips of tendon from the frog's rear legs. Now he had to find out if his containers would hold water for any length of time. He filled both skins with water from his heel-scooped saucer, hung them on a withered shrub near his camp, and went to sleep.

With morning, both skins were as he had left them the previous night. If there had been any loss through leakage, it was too small to be noticed. Balulu was elated. His major problem thus solved, he set out to dig more frogs.

He now had a plan which, while not a guarantee of success, did promise that travel in the immediate future would be far better than it had been. He would stay here long enough to dig a great many frogs. Their sun-dried flesh would assure food for Warrigal and himself. The water they contained, stored in their own skins, would hold off the pangs of thirst.

Four great frogs dangling from his left hand, Balulu returned to camp and suffered a rude shock. The frogskin canteens had held water well enough during the cool night, but the blazing sun had now shriveled them to iron-hard parchment. They hung where Balulu had left them, but they resembled nothing more than a pair of withered twigs. Neither retained a single drop of moisture.

It was a bitter disappointment, but one that had to be faced. Balulu was determined to go on, and if necessary he would do so without water. But food he would and could have.

All four frogs he had dug were distended with

water. Casting about for some way to conserve it until he and Warrigal were thirsty, Balulu decided against his heel-scooped saucer. The fierce sun would be certain to dry up any water that did not seep into the ground. Then he noticed one of the hollow tree trunks he had used for his fire last night. The upper part of the trunk had burned away, leaving only a hollow stump with a solid bottom at the base.

For a moment he stared at it in disbelief. Then, in imagination, he saw the thin-shelled stump, filled with water, the open end plugged with a piece of wood. To gather as many similar sections as he could carry, he had only to look. They could be burned down to the size he wanted, and further hollowed out by the sharp head of his stabbing stick.

He had found his containers!

CHAPTER NINE

Twelve times had the sun risen since Balulu turned his back on the dry lake with its mud-burrowing frogs. On this mid-morning of the twelfth day Balulu was climbing a long, low hill, while Warrigal coursed through the nearby scrub on one of his endless side excursions in search of anything that moved.

Two hollow sections of tree, one half filled with water, hung by frogskin thongs from Balulu's shoulder. His pouch still contained a small store of sun-dried frog flesh. The supplies carried from the lake had been supplemented with some food and water found along the way. Both were still scarce, but the past four days had brought them through a less desolate land. The drought had reached here, but not with the same prolonged intensity. Almost no warm-blooded game lingered in the area, but there was a reasonable number of snakes and lizards, and Warrigal had occasionally run down and killed one of the crest-tailed desert rats.

Furthermore, Balulu knew that other tribes had once lived here, at least for a time. He had found a cave eroded out of the side of a rocky escarpment, on the back of which had been painted the likenesses of men. They had had weapons in their hands, but whether these meant hunting or war Balulu had not been able to tell. In any event, he had been keeping a sharp watch the last few days.

Topping the brow of the hill, Balulu saw something that made him stop in amazement. He stared down the slope at a small tree, a dwarf variety of mountain-dwelling eucalyptus. By customary standards it was singularly unimpressive: its topmost branches were no higher than the top of Balulu's head, it was stunted, and prevailing winds had given the trunk a permanent list. But its branches bore live green leaves!

In a daze of mingled awe and dumb wonder, Balulu emerged from his trance and walked slowly toward the tree. He kept unwavering eyes upon it, fearful that the little tree was either a mirage that would presently fade from sight or the creation of some evil spirit. Finally reaching the tree, Balulu stood motionless and stared at it until he found the nerve to grasp a leaf between thumb and forefinger. The leaf was pliant, green, alive, exactly like the leaves Balulu remembered. His spirits soared as the meaning of those green leaves became clear to him.

Lifting his eyes, Balulu saw a range of rolling hills, the near ones rocky and bleak and the far ones wrapped in a shimmering haze that his gaze could not pierce. Until he came near enough to see for himself what lay upon them, he could not know for certain what they contained. But one green tree surely pointed the way to more. Somewhere in the mountains that lay before him he would again walk among green groves. The valleys would be well watered, with many grassy meadows where herds of kangaroos and wallabies grew fat.

Balulu knelt in the thin shade of the little tree. Gravely and carefully he used the point of his stabbing stick to trace the symbol of the Dingo Totem on the trunk near its base. Rising, he touched the trunk with the extended fingers of his left hand and intoned the spoken ritual which may be heard only by those already of the Dingo Totem or those who are about to join it. The ceremony completed, he felt a satisfaction and a serenity of mind such as he had seldom known. Unorthodox though it might be to make a tree his brother, there was no other way to express his gratitude. The tree *was* his brother. In showing Balulu that he was on the right path, it had served him beyond measure.

As though approving the initiation ceremony, Warrigal came in from his wanderings and stretched out in the shade of the little tree.

When they resumed their journey, Balulu did

so with a light heart and eager steps. The desolate valley in which he presently found himself was bleak and boulder-strewn, but because he had fresh hope, even the bleakness seemed a promise of better things to come. Halting while there was still sufficient daylight to find a sheltered camp and gather wood, Balulu shared a few morsels of sun-dried frog meat with Warrigal and divided a portion of the remaining water with his brother.

The dingo lying beside him, Balulu stared into his fire and tried to interpret the images appearing there. Watching the various shapes the flames might assume and reading significance into them was a habit of long standing. Where Balulu had before seen sun-bleached skeletons, dry water holes, and hunger-lean men and dingoes, now he saw herds of fat kangaroos and wallabies, flocks of parrots, cassowaries whose nest and tasty eggs invited discovery, honey ants, plump possums. The whole parade of life as a hunter would wish it seemed to pass through Balulu's fire. For the first time in many nights he stretched out to sleep with an easy and untroubled mind. The images

that had danced in his fire transferred to his imagination, so that even while sleeping he saw
game more plentiful than he had ever known it.

When he awakened during the night, he did so
instantly and completely. It was a hunter's awak-
ening, without any lingering drowsiness between
sound sleep and full alertness. Presently the far-
off, wailing moan that had penetrated Balulu's
sleep came a second time, and he listened with
awed delight. The wild cry in the night was almost as astonishing as the green tree, and fully as
significant.

A wild dingo was calling its mate, but the sound
was as different from the whimpering dingoes that
haunted his tribe's night camp as the green tree
was different from a shriveled bush. This dingo
was no half-starved scavenger who hoped for a
scrap of food and would do anything to get it. The
sound was wild and proud, as it should be. It
boasted of a kill already made, and of the hunter's
ability to defend the quarry until the absent mate
came to share it.

Warrigal, too, had heard the cry of the wild

dingo, and was sitting tensely erect, head raised and ears pricked forward.

"Do you hear, Warrigal?" Balulu whispered, his hand on the furry neck. "It is our wild brother. He welcomes us."

Balulu went back to sleep with the comforting assurance that the presence of wild dingoes no longer meant danger. With other game to be had for the hunting, no dingo would ever attack a man.

With morning, Balulu awakened a second time after the most restful night he had had since he left the tribe. There was no longer the least shred of doubt that he was on the right track. The cry of the dingo had confirmed every promise made by the green-leaved tree. Where there was a hunting dingo, there was something to hunt. Opening his pouch, Balulu shared all the rest of his dried frog meat with Warrigal and together they drank half their remaining water. Yesterday morning he would not have considered it, but now Balulu had complete faith in the signs he had seen and heard.

The day's journey was not an hour old when it

brought another positive sign that conditions were about to change. High on the side of a treeless slope dotted with great red boulders, a trickle of water oozed from beneath one of the boulders, gathered in a pebbly pool, then overflowed in a tiny stream that continued down the hill into a steeply pitched gully. Side by side, Balulu and Warrigal stretched out beside the pool and drank until they could hold no more.

"Brother, we have come to a good land," Balulu told Warrigal happily. "Our bellies are filled with water, and if we follow where it leads, they will soon be filled with meat."

Hurrying along the course of the little stream, they followed the gully to a precipice over which the wandering rill disappeared. From the top of the ledge, Balulu looked down on the scene he had come so far to find.

In the valley beneath him, the little rill became part of a larger stream that sparkled in the sun and made a lazy bend to disappear in the distance. Lush green meadows bordering the stream were alive with big red kangaroos and their smaller, smoke-blue females. Beyond these meadows were low and gentle hills, dotted with green trees that seemed filled with kea parrots and brightly colored, crested cockatoos. Beneath the trees Balulu could see emus feeding on fallen fruit.

Looking upon this unbelievable scene, Balulu knew that his quest was ended. As the little green tree had promised, he had left the land of drought and hunger behind and had come to a country of such abundance as he had never seen.

CHAPTER TEN

Part way up a gently sloping knoll, a little spring bubbled out between two lichen-encrusted boulders and trickled through a grove of gum trees to a meeting with the stream. Stretched out in the shade, Warrigal sprawled full length like any big dog, his tail straight behind him and head resting on his fore paws. The dingo's nose wriggled and his paws twitched as he relaxed in the full enjoyment of some happy canine dream.

On the other side of the little rill, Balulu was busy skinning a fat kangaroo. As the limp skin fell away from the firm flesh, he spread the skin on the ground and on it began slicing the meat into strips. Despite the primitive knife that the flint head of his stabbing stick made, in hands so skilled the work proceeded smoothly and swiftly. He had been at it several days now, dressing out kangaroo meat in strips for curing in the sun. He had already made a new skin pouch, and had cut enough strips of bark to bind together the supplies he intended to take back over the mountains. Beside his weapons and canteens of water, his burden would consist of as much sun-cured kangaroo meat as he was able to pack.

It was an amendment to his original plan. Leaving the tribe, his only thought had been to look for a better hunting ground. If he found one, he had planned to return and guide his starving people to it. But experience had taught him much.

While at the dry lake with its mud-burrowing frogs, he had concentrated on the need for finding some practical way to carry water and finally recognized a hollow trunk as his solution. Need had also directed him to fill his pouch with sun-cured frog flesh. Because he had food and water, and therefore need not stop to hunt either, he made the rest of his journey in half the time he might otherwise have needed. Clearly his return trip could be greatly expedited in the same manner, and further shortened because he knew the way.

The meat finally removed from one of the kangaroo's leg bones, Balulu tossed the bone to Warrigal. The big dingo raised his head, blinked sleepy eyes, and sniffed at the offering. A grin flitted across Balulu's lips. He and Warrigal had endured much hunger in coming here, but there had been a surfeit of everything since they had arrived. Never had Balulu even dreamed of such hunting.

Great kangaroos and their smaller cousins, the wallabies, swarmed in every meadow. There were wild turkeys, a variety of possums, a rabbit-sized kind of bandicoot that Balulu had never seen before, with leathery ears and a long, pointed snout. Every tree was home to several kinds of birds, some familiar, some strange, and to the bushy-tailed, squirrel-like gliders, that could soar from tree to tree almost as easily as the birds. Of course there were the predators, too: wild dingoes, thy-

lacines, and Tasmanian devils, which looked very
fierce, but spent their time peacefully hunting the
stream banks for frogs and crabs. In a land of such
plenty, predators posed no threat if one trod war-
ily near the thylacines.

Most amazing to Balulu was the lack of wari-
ness on the part of these wild creatures, particu-
larly the kangaroos. Though Balulu could remember that on rare occasions the Desert People's
hunters had found game easy to kill because it
lacked fear and could be approached, kangaroos
had always been a test for any hunter. To come
near enough to kill or wound one with a boomerang was not always easy, and only when ambushed could they be brought down with spears.
The tribe's hunters had always earned their kangaroo meat.

Balulu had never known hunting such as this.
Rather than have to stalk to come within boomerang range of a kangaroo, here he could always
walk openly to within a hundred yards or even
nearer. The kangaroos seemed to consider themselves safe if they kept only a short distance away.

The valley should have been a hunter's paradise, and except for one puzzlingly uncertain factor it was.

Balulu had taken for granted the fact that, if he should stumble across a worthwhile hunting ground, it would already be in the possession of some alien tribe. He had been certain that they would not welcome a stranger, but he had not known what to do about such a situation. It would have to depend on circumstances when and if he met them.

Now he found himself both puzzled and worried because, so far, he had not run across any signs of other human hunters, except a few spots containing ashes from very old camp sites. This was far more disquieting than more recent evidences would have been. There was no question that a land as rich in game as this one was both known and claimed. What had happened to the makers of those old fires? All tribes were wanderers, but they always came back to places offering such an abundance of food and water as this one did. The mysterious absence of signs of a recent visit meant that he must perpetually be alert for unpleasant surprises. But of what kind?

Balulu had safeguarded himself in every way he knew or could devise. Since there was little danger from wild beasts—at least those he had seen—and the weather was mild, he kept no night fire at all and built only a very small blaze for cooking his meat. That was always just after nightfall, for the smoke from a daytime fire could be seen from far away. He always kindled it on a smooth rock in a shallow place well out from the stream bank. Balulu's cooking finished, he spilled the ashes into the stream and submerged the rock in deeper water until he needed it again.

Hunting young kangaroos and wallabies only, he restricted himself exclusively to smaller animals that could be picked up and carried from wherever they fell to the grove of trees near the spring. When he had dressed out the meat, Balulu returned the offal, bones, and skin to the scene of the kill. There wandering dingoes or thylacines were sure to find and pick over the remains, thereby making it appear that they had

killed the animal. Also, this system kept predators from being attracted to Balulu's camp among
the trees, so that he and Warrigal could sleep in
peace.

Thus Balulu had taken every possible precau-
tion, but it was impossible to conceal his daytime
hunting activities. There were some risks he could
not avoid.

Balulu cut the last of the meat from the kangaroo bones. Since he must pack everything, every
inedible ounce was excess weight. He sliced away
all muscle and tendons. With an unlimited supply
of game from which to choose, he could afford to
be particular. When he had sliced all the meat
into thin strips, Balulu strung the pieces on supple
green twigs which he had been careful to take
from a tree in the very center of the grove. He
wanted no hostile eyes to detect torn branches
when they first scanned the valley.

Rising, Balulu wrapped all unwanted portions
of the kangaroo in the limp hide and carried it out
in the meadow. Returning, he bound his meat-
laden twigs together with a strip of hide and car-

ried the bundle up the hill, beyond the spring. Laying each twig separately, checking to make sure there was an air space between every strip of meat, Balulu arranged them on a flat rock whose surface was well hidden by surrounding grass. He took a handful of ashes from his pouch and sprinkled them over the meat. Exposed on the rock, the meat would be cured by the sun, and would lose half its weight in the process. The ashes would ward off hungry wild prowlers that might fear nothing else but always feared fire and whatever reminded them of fire.

Straightening the grass as he did so, he backed away from the rock.

Even though he spared no effort to hide what he was doing, this was by far Balulu's greatest risk. Tall grass might hide the meat, but ashes would not repel a fire-loving tame dingo should some hunter happen to pass with one. For that matter, the hunter's own nose might tell him of the meat and he would certainly investigate. But Balulu knew of no way to avoid such risks. To dry the meat meant that he could carry twice as much.

He made a mental tabulation of the various caches he had on hidden rocks; there was almost enough. Another day and another kangaroo would provide a full load. Allowing time to let the last of it dry, he could leave.

When he came back there would be enough of his tribe to meet force with force, if necessary.

Four days later, Balulu strung the last of his dried meat supply on a strip of kangaroo skin and knelt to bind the various strips into a compact, bark-covered bundle. He balanced it on both sides with water-filled containers and swung the load to his shoulders. It was heavier than he had thought it would be, and he gave a foreboding thought to the fact that weight seems to increase as the body grows weary. But he was rested and well fed and he would abandon none of it. As he and Warrigal ate and drank along the way, the load would become light enough as the days slipped behind.

Balulu turned his back on this green land where life abounded and set off on the long journey that would return him to the parched desert and the

hungry Desert People. But he had gone only a
short distance up the stream when Warrigal
snarled a warning. Seconds later, a flashing boomerang whirled past and cut through the top of a
small mulga tree growing a few feet to one side.
In startled disbelief, Balulu turned to look behind
him.

Not more than a hundred yards away, the naked upper body of a man was framed above the
tall grass. His hair, bound with white shells in a
style totally unfamiliar to Balulu, stamped him as
an alien, as did the red and yellow ocher that
streaked his body in startling contrast to the black
and white pigments known to the Desert People.
His left hand gripped his spears and his right was
poised, ready to throw another boomerang.

Balulu half raised his own boomerang, but at
once lowered it. His chances of bringing the stranger down were good, but by no means assured. If
he threw and missed, there would be no opportunity to recover his boomerang. Before he sacri-
ficed a weapon, he must be sure of a kill.

The hunter's second boomerang came spinning

toward him and missed by a yard more than the
first. Although the stranger was throwing at ad-
mittedly long range, not even an apprentice hunter should miss by that much. And the man was no
apprentice, with those paint markings of full tribal maturity. Balulu now knew the solution to one
mystery. Those kangaroos that had considered
themselves at safe distance from him had been
hunted by men who could not strike with telling
effect at such a distance.

All this flashed through Balulu's mind as he
turned and ran, as though in panicky flight. Lad-
en as Balulu was, he knew the stranger could close
the distance between them rapidly. Presently he
whirled suddenly and made ready to throw his
boomerang. The hunter he had hoped would be
lured within close range by a supposedly terrified
victim, had dropped out of sight as completely as
though he had never appeared. Even though he
might have done nothing more than throw himself down in the tall grass, his sudden disappearance was even more unnerving than his surprising
and unexpected appearance.

Regardless of how badly he threw a boomerang, there was no questioning his ability to stalk.
That he had been able to come so close in the first
place, and remain undetected, was sufficient proof
of that. Undoubtedly he had intended to come
much nearer, within certain killing distance before he threw his boomerang, and would have succeeded if Warrigal's snarl hadn't warned Balulu.
The hunter had chanced what he must have
known was a wild shot only because he knew he
was discovered.

But where was he now? Was he hidden or
hadn't he pursued at all? Trying to find out, Balulu circled into a favorable wind. He studied his
back trail, trying to analyze what the stranger
might have done. He could see nothing, and knew
from Warrigal's actions that the dingo had caught
no trace of human scent.

Balulu could be certain of nothing except that
there was no present pursuit. That eliminated the
need for immediate swift flight. It would be better to set a reasonable speed at first; there was
every probability of enough running later on.

The fact that the hunter had disappeared did not delude Balulu into thinking that there would be no pursuit. On the contrary, the stranger's disappearance was to be expected from a hunter of experience. Only reckless fools invited their own destruction by pressing hotly after dangerous game. The hunter knew very well that Balulu was also armed, so it was the right time and place for a wise hunter to fall back on strategy.

What strategy? Balulu faced an enormous handicap in lacking full knowledge of the terrain; he knew only what he had seen. But the hunter was undoubtedly on his home grounds, and knew them as intimately as Balulu knew his own tribe's desert territory. A knowledge of short cuts, and an acquaintance with geographical quirks that could be utilized, were factors that the stranger would use to his advantage.

Balulu decided that his pursuer—or pursuers, for there might be more than one—would linger far enough behind to avoid any fight until the odds were in his favor; that would be the time the stranger would strike. Lack of skill with a boom-

erang was no good reason to think that the hunter was stupid. To assume so might be fatal.

Despite the disadvantage imposed by his scan-
ty knowledge of the terrain, Balulu planned as
wisely as possible. The obvious and easiest course
for any fugitive lay up the stream bed, following
the available water as far as possible before striking out toward the dry desert. Thinking of this, it
occurred to Balulu that he possessed one decided
advantage which tilted the balance in his favor
because the pursuer couldn't possibly know about
it. Because of the water he carried, he was inde-
pendent of the stream. The instant the thought
presented itself, Balulu translated it into action.

A half mile short of the cliff from which he and
Warrigal had first looked out on the green land,
he made a right-angle turn that brought him to
the crest of one of the flanking hills. He slipped
down the far slope, descended into the valley,
and climbed the next hill. There he turned back
in the direction he really wanted to go.

It was a maneuver that promised a margin of
safety. Though his tracks remained for anyone

whose eyes could read a trail, even the keenest tracker would need time to work them out and would be able to follow at no more than half Balulu's speed. Nor could anyone track at all after night fell. Balulu could certainly keep his lead on any tracker and therein lay his greatest hope. Furthermore, the arid country he was heading for was a forbidding one. Balulu hoped that the pursuer, or pursuers, would cling to his trail only as long as they could do so without separating themselves from assured food and water.

Because he wanted to make it as hard as possible for any tracker by putting a maximum number of miles behind him, Balulu now alternately walked and dog trotted. He came out of the last of the trees into the higher and more desolate mountains and turned to study his back trail. Nobody appeared and there was no sign of life.

Somewhat reassured, but taking nothing for granted, Balulu went on. For his night's camp he chose the crest of a steep-sided spire where there was scarcely room enough for Warrigal and himself. He felt reasonably safe here; one man on top could repulse many trying to climb the sides. Balulu and Warrigal ate some of the newly dried meat, drank a little water, and settled down to a fireless camp. Throughout the night there was no alarm.

With morning, Balulu could again see nothing and felt sure that he was at least temporarily safe. He concluded that the strange hunter was either as unskilled in tracking as he was in throwing a boomerang and hadn't the ability to follow, or he had been content with merely chasing Balulu away.

CHAPTER ELEVEN

Though signs indicated that the hunter either was not pursuing at all or was having so much trouble working out the trail that he needn't be feared, Balulu had no intention of relaxing his guard. The crest of the spire upon which he and Warrigal had passed the night reared many feet taller than any nearby high point, thus offering a sweeping panorama of the lower country through which they had traveled. Balulu turned for an intensive study of his back trail.

Holding perfectly still, for to move was to invite attention, he squatted on his haunches with one hand laid warningly on Warrigal's furry ruff.

The green land was far behind and half hidden by thin streamers of mist that floated out of the warm valleys. The bleak heights near at hand were mist free and so clear that a lizard might have been seen if it had flicked its tail.

Balulu saw nothing. These high, arid lands seemed as empty of life as the green country had been teeming with it. Certain that there was either nobody on his trail, or that he had nothing to fear from any tracker so inept that he was not far enough along to be sighted by this time, Balulu turned to study the region that lay in front of him.

Some distance ahead was a nest of craggy peaks with sides so smooth and steep that it seemed as if nothing except a fly could find a foothold upon them. Through the peaks Balulu traced out the only path he could possibly take unless he decided to back-track and find a whole new route. As it approached the peaks, the broad basin he had been traveling pinched in to a sheer-walled canyon that slanted steeply upwards. Near the summit, where the peaks leveled out to a barren pla-

teau, the canyon became a shallow gully so narrow that at this distance it looked as though a
man could reach from one rim to the other.

Balulu frowned uneasily. He must cross the
mountains and obviously he could do so only by
way of the walled canyon and the narrow gully.
But he had an instinctive distrust of such places;
both seemed too much like a trap. Still, he had already crossed these same mountains once, and
knew from firsthand observation that no humans
lived in them. Turning for one final glance toward
the rear, the direction from which any pursuit
would have to come, Balulu decided that he had
nothing to fear. Besides, the shortest way lay
ahead. If he back-tracked to avoid the canyon and
gully, he must return almost all the way to the
green valleys before choosing a different route
and that meant the loss of precious time.

His decision made, he and Warrigal half slid
and half climbed down the spire. As soon as they
were at the bottom, Warrigal shook himself and
enjoyed a luxurious roll in a bed of sand. Balulu
lingered a moment, again uneasy about the path

he'd chosen and once more wondering if it would not be wise to find another. Then he shrugged his pack to a more comfortable position and resolutely faced toward the canyon. There was no assurance of safety anywhere. Regardless of where he went, he must risk something and there was no guarantee that any other route would be better.

While Warrigal trotted from side to side sniffing at every crevice, cranny, and bush that struck his fancy, Balulu set a brisk pace that was in accord with suddenly high spirits. He had not only done what he had set out to do, but he was bringing proof of his discovery back to the Desert People. If he and Warrigal found no other food and must live entirely from the pack he was carrying, they would still return to the tribe with most of the kangaroo meat. As food, it would not be much, but as proof of a land of plenty, it would be salvation to his people.

Now, at long last, he was very sure. Not even the forlorn tableland held any terrors for one who carried a plentiful supply of food and water. Nor was there a faint possibility of anything save a rousing welcome when he came back to the tribe. Though he'd flouted Rono's authority, no punishment could await anyone who brought food and a promise of an unlimited supply of more. Rono himself, if he hoped to remain chief, would have to pardon any bearer of such proof of plenty.

Best of all, the Desert People would again have promise of an abundance of everything necessary for life. Having it, they would again be able to think and act as befitted humans.

A good-sized lizard flicked across the line of march and Balulu instinctively raised his boomerang. He lowered it without throwing. At any other time the lizard would have been a welcome supplement to the food stocks; the less kangaroo meat Warrigal and Balulu ate, the more there would be for the tribe. Because he was still uneasy about the walled canyon and the narrow gully, and was anxious to have them both behind him as soon as possible, Balulu did not want to add to the already heavy load he was carrying.

Seeing the lizard, Warrigal pricked up interested ears and rushed it. Alarmed, the darting lizard disappeared in a crevice six inches ahead of the racing dingo. With all the bouncy zest of a puppy, Warrigal began to scratch at the opening.

Balulu noted the action approvingly. Neither he nor Warrigal had had any spirits to spare during their journey to the green country. But all the food they could eat had restored the vitality of both and given Balulu additional reason to believe he could shorten the return journey by many days. He was no longer the half-starved hunter who had left the tribe.

Reaching the canyon, Balulu halted briefly, then went ahead, chiding himself for acting like a boy hunter who has learned just enough to imagine danger wherever he went. Except that it was cooler than the broad basin, for the sun was not yet high enough to strike here fully, the canyon was no different from the plain he had just left, Balulu told himself. There was no hint of danger. Still, all Balulu's training as a hunter made him uneasy about entering such a place; he liked at all times to be aware of exactly what lay ahead.

The steep-walled canyon offered him and Warrigal no hint of any scent or sound except those which came from behind. The canyon acted as a flue; its walls and floor formed a route up which the wind blew constantly but in one direction only, toward the peaks. The keenest-scented dingo that ever raced along a wallaby's trail could not have walked up the canyon and learned in advance what he would find.

Increasingly anxious to be out of such a confining place, Balulu trotted steadily on. He was no longer concerned about pursuit, and tried to re-assure himself that no danger could possibly lie ahead. He saw no tracks, no sign of life, nor did Warrigal show interest in anything along the way. There was nothing at all to impede their progress, apart from the fact that the floor pitched more steeply the farther they traveled, and made climbing harder.

Finally Balulu climbed the last and steepest pitch and found himself within the mouth of the narrow gully. His anxiety ebbed away.

So near the summit, the wind whistled up the canyon behind him and whirled into the gully with substantially increased force. But the high rock walls of the canyon gave way to much lower ones in the gully, which ended on the high plateau only an easy spear cast away.

Balulu quickened his pace. The trap was almost behind and he was anxious to be rid of it, even though he knew he must then face the desolate high plateau and the full heat of the sun. No matter. He would feel at ease only when the four points of the compass again lay open before him, and he could see in any direction.

Balulu trotted out of the gully. Just as he left it behind, a bristled Warrigal leaped in front of him, hackles raised and fangs bared. One rumbling snarl followed another as the dingo stopped and braced himself beside his brother.

Completely surprised, for a moment Balulu could only stare in disbelief.

No more than thirty feet away, his lower body hidden by the boulder behind which he had been hiding, stood a man. There was no doubt that it was the hunter whom Balulu had met in the green valley. His hair was bound precisely the same, down to the last white shell. The same red and yellow streaks of ocher decorated his chest and right arm. There was only one thing that differed from the first time Balulu had seen the stranger.

This time the man's lifted right hand gripped a *womera* in which a spear was ready. The way he balanced *womera* and spear, and his stance as he prepared to cast, told Balulu all he had to know. The man might not be skilled in throwing boomerangs, but he had nothing to learn about spears.

Too late, Balulu realized that he had blundered into the very trap he had feared all along. It was a cunning ambush, so craftily planned and carried out that Balulu could not suppress admiration even though he stared into the face of death in the form of the poised spear.

The hunter was indeed a worthy foe. With no need to run himself breathless or take unnecessary risks, he had out-thought and out-planned Balulu on every count. Putting himself in Balulu's place, even reading his thoughts, the hunter had obviously followed the trail only to where Balulu had made his right-angle turn. There had been no need to do more, for Balulu's move had revealed his whole plan. Intimately acquainted with his own country, the hunter had known that Balulu must eventually appear at the mouth of this gully and had taken a short cut to it. Even as he was wishing that he had obeyed his deepest instincts and turned back to find another route, Balulu found comfort in the thought that, since he must lose, it would be to a hunter he could respect.

Other naked bodies rose from behind other boulders until Balulu counted seven. But only the hunter had shells in his hair and only he wore the ocher stripes. Obviously he was a leader in charge of apprentice hunters; the other six were scarcely more than boys.

The leader still stood motionless, spear poised in *womera*, ready for throwing. Did he intend to take Balulu prisoner, for later tribal punishment? If he was going to die, Balulu preferred to die fighting. Tightening his grip on his boomerang, he took a sharp, calculating second look at the leader.

Spear and *womera* were rigid in the hand that

held them. Boomerang in ready position, Balulu faced his enemy across a distance so short that, if weapons were launched, somebody must die. But both stood still, each staring at the other.

The hunter spoke. "I am Gallum, of the Valley People, and I know now that I cannot kill you. But unless you lay down your weapons and become my captive, you will surely be killed by these six others."

"I will lay my weapons down, Gallum," Balulu said. "I, Balulu, of the Desert People, will become your captive."

Balulu dropped his weapons on the ground. He could do no less. In that fleeting interval when he and Gallum faced each other, before their weapons were hurled, each had seen in the other's tattooing the distinctive symbol that may adorn only those of the Dingo Totem.

They were brothers.

CHAPTER TWELVE

The six young hunters who formed an armed circle around Balulu tried to make themselves appear properly warlike by wearing fierce scowls. On his part, Balulu was loftily scornful, and insulted all six guards by pretending that he was not even aware of their presence. He was in no immediate danger and knew it.

If they had dared, any one of the six young hunters would have been glad to kill Balulu at any time since his capture. But they didn't dare. As Gallum's prisoner, Balulu had been entitled to receive the brotherly treatment which any member of the Dingo Totem must bestow upon any other member, including captured enemies. Now that they were back in the green country of the Valley People, all the young guards could do was make the most of the honor of guarding the captive while Gallum and other leading members of his people decided Balulu's ultimate fate.

An arm's length away, Warrigal lay so quietly that he seemed to be sleeping. But Balulu knew that his four-footed brother was wide awake and alert. Warrigal was ready for any new development in this unusual situation.

Balulu stretched, shifted his position to one side, and was instantly stopped by a spear point pricking his chest. He gave an ostentatious yawn. The six young hunters were completely responsible for preventing an escape, but they would answer to Gallum if they killed or even hurt his captive, and Balulu knew it. What he didn't know was what kind of fate would face him if the deliberating Council of Elders found any way to relieve Gallum of his pledges to the Dingo Totem. Not knowing the customs of the Valley People, Balulu had no idea what was in store for him.

Since nothing had happened as yet and Balulu saw no good reason for worrying, he let his thoughts take him back to his capture, and the three days that had elapsed since.

Though from the first the six young hunters had made no attempt to conceal their unfavorable opinions of capturing a trespasser who could be easily and permanently disposed of by a spear point, Gallum had made it clear that the prisoner was not to be harmed. Balulu had not even been bound. Stripped of all weapons and with six boys on guard, each one knowing that any attempt to escape gave them an automatic opportunity to kill the prisoner, Balulu realized that there was no hope of getting away.

While not overly friendly, Gallum had been entirely willing to talk with his prisoner. Balulu had violated the land of the Valley People, Gallum told him, and would have been found out much sooner except that he had entered a remote section of their country. Hunters seldom went there. Though the hunting was good, it was just as good in other sections, and this particular valley Balulu had found was isolated by a high and difficult range of hills.

Gallum had appeared, on the very day Balulu planned to leave, because he was in charge of the six boys who were undertaking the next step that would qualify them as Senior Hunters. The step, a decidedly practical one, consisted of journeying to a remote section and proving their ability to live off the country the entire way.

The Valley People depended almost entirely on spears, said Gallum, because spears became their most dependable weapon when their ancestor, Abishe, revealed how to fashion them from hardwood strips split from the mulga tree. Later Abishe had taught his people how to make and use the *womera,* to lengthen the distance their spears could be cast. That had been very long ago, soon after the beginning of time, when the Valley People were very few, very weak, and so in want of everything that all would have perished had not Abishe appeared to lead them.

Without further elaboration, Gallum had furnished a practical illustration to his story by catch-

ing up a light, ten-foot spear, casting it farther
than the best spearsman in Balulu's tribe could
have done, and scoring a perfect hit on a clump of
spinifex grass that he had chosen for a target. He
looked questioningly at Balulu, as though challenging him to equal the shot. Balulu thought
wistfully of his boomerangs.

"That was indeed a good cast," Balulu said ad-
miringly. "The spears of my people are shorter
and would not carry that far. But my boomerang
would."

"That may be true," Gallum admitted, "for
your boomerangs are heavier than ours. But no
boomerang could hit the clump at that distance."
It was plain that he thought Balulu was boasting,
knowing that his captors would not let him get
his hands on his weapons.

A spear was all the weapon anyone needed,
Gallum went on. A reasonably good spearsman
with some knowledge of stalking would never be
hungry, since he could have as much meat as he
needed for the taking. Remembering the valley
kangaroos that had waited for him to come with-

in easy boomerang range, Balulu did not challenge that statement.

"But when you first saw me," Balulu persisted,
"you were carrying a boomerang, and threw it. If
a spear is such a brother to your hand, why did
you not use it then instead?"

"I was not expecting a stranger in that valley,"
Gallum answered thoughtfully. "I was looking for
mulga trees, and carrying a boomerang to knock
down seeds from the high branches. When your
dingo snarled, I had no time to change weapons.
It was lucky for you, because I did not know then
that you were a brother, and might have killed
you. I think our Dingo Totem willed that I should
have been carrying a boomerang and not a spear."

Thinking over their return to the green country
of the Valley People, Balulu realized that even
Gallum was in no position to tell him what was to
come. His captor wouldn't know himself until he
had consulted with the Valley People's Council of
Elders.

That consultation had been in progress since a
waning moon left sufficient darkness to keep oth-

er, lesser, eyes from looking upon the various council members as they slipped away to their sacred meeting place. The sun had since risen and swung so far along its daily course that the long shadows of early morning had become the very short ones that precede mid-day. There was no hint of what, if anything, had been decided.

Again managing to ignore his six young guards by refusing to acknowledge they existed, Balulu looked about the grassy meadow in which he was being held captive.

In common with other Australian aborigines, the Valley People not only had no fixed dwellings, but so far Balulu had seen no evidence that they even resorted to the hastily erected and casually abandoned brush or grass shelters which his tribe sometimes used to keep off the cold night wind. But though the Valley People were hunters, therefore wanderers who must follow the game, they were as well sheltered and as settled as he imagined any people could be.

Gallum had not lied. Even though the country of the Valley People that Balulu had seen was lit-

tle more than half as big as the Desert People's
home lands, it was fantastically wealthy. Number-
ing about four hundred in all, at Balulu's guess, it
seemed to him that these strangers had so much
of everything that they could take all they wanted
and still make no difference in the remainder.
They had enough for five times as many people,
he was sure, and no need to wander long distances to have abundance at hand.

Asking Gallum how they managed to keep all
of it for themselves when there was always some
hungry tribe bent on using as much force as necessary to induce sharing any neighboring abundance, Balulu had learned that the eastern border
of the Valley People's land was a lesser country
where game was never plentiful and often scarce.
It was inhabited by two small tribes that would
never become much bigger simply because there
was not enough food for a large population. The
two tribes were constantly at war with each other,
which further served to keep both in a state of
weakness. Neither tribe, nor the two combined,
had enough warriors to worry the Valley People.

Bordering this poor country, Gallum said, mountain ranges that he believed nobody could cross discouraged any people who lived on the far side and might be inclined to trespass. Until Balulu arrived, not only had nobody yet come from the west but the Valley People had supposed nobody even lived there. They thought the high bleak plateaus on their own western border reached to the ends of the earth.

Balulu let his eyes stray to the trees that bordered the meadow. The women, children, and all male members of the Valley People who were not engaged in guarding Balulu or deciding his fate, lingered there and avoided any indication that they even knew a captive was at hand. Doubtless they were under strict orders, for they must have been curious about this stranger from the western desert country. Balulu looked at Warrigal, tied to a small gum tree a few feet away. He and his brother could not help each other now, he reflected, even though their totem had saved their lives when Gallum had first seen the symbol on Balulu's chest.

As he had done a dozen times, Balulu considered his chances of escape. There was nothing to indicate they had improved, which meant they did not exist. Even if he escaped the six young guards, he must then reckon with all the others. If he managed to elude them, it would be only temporary. With no weapons and deep in the land of the Valley People, he wouldn't have a chance.

Moreover, escaping without food or weapons might be a worse fate than whatever awaited him here. Though the council's decision had not been reached, or at least had not been made known, there was a possibility that it would lean in his favor. Until he knew what the council decided it would be best to do nothing.

Partly for lack of something better to do, and partly because anything he learned about the Valley People now might prove to be useful knowledge at some future date, Balulu looked back to the people among the trees. To his astonishment, though all had been going about their affairs a few minutes ago, now there was nobody in sight. Even the cooking fires must have been extinguished, because smoke was no longer rising. Since it was impossible for so many people to have run away, it followed that all had hidden themselves. Why?

Balulu stirred uneasily. Shadows had grown so short as to be almost non-existent. In a very short time it would be exactly high noon.

A few seconds later the six young guards stiffened, grunted to each other, and got to their feet. Each raised his spear so the shaft pointed toward the ground and the head rested on the bridge of his nose. They stopped scowling and glaring at Balulu, which they had been doing for the past many hours, and stared fixedly ahead. They did not make the slightest motion. To all outward appearances, they even ceased breathing.

Warrigal growled softly and looked toward the head of the valley. Following his brother's gaze, Balulu saw the reason for such abrupt ceremony on the part of his guards. The council must have reached a verdict, and, exactly at high noon was returning to give it.

Twenty in all, the Council of Elders came in

double file with the most notable and influential first and thereafter arranged in descending order of importance. Gallum himself headed the left-hand column. Leading the right, wearing so many cassowary plumes that his hair could scarcely be seen, was the High Chief of the Valley People. The rest were ornamented in various ways, according to totem and positions in the tribe. All of them carried themselves with solemn dignity, which became even more strongly sensed when the procession halted about fifteen feet from Balulu. After a moment, Gallum alone came forward. With his outstretched hand he offered Balulu one of his own boomerangs.

Gallum said gravely, "In keeping with my pledges to the Dingo Totem, I return a brother's weapon."

Balulu turned puzzled eyes on the boomerang. All members of the Dingo Totem were indeed pledged never to destroy another's weapons, but why was Gallum returning only one boomerang? Where were his spears, his other boomerang, his stabbing stick?

Now Gallum moved back to his place in the council, and the High Chief stepped forward.

"Stranger," he said solemnly, "you have told Gallum that you come from the land to the west. Is this true?"

"It is true," Balulu said, facing him fearlessly. "I am Balulu of the Desert People, whose country lies to the west."

"How many are the Desert People?"

"Ten times the number of my fingers," Balulu told him.

"Why did you come here? Who guided you?"

"I came seeking food for my people, and was guided by the spirit of the Dingo Totem."

At mention of the Dingo Totem, a low murmur ran through the Council of Elders but why, Balulu could not guess. The High Chief raised his hand, and the murmur died.

"You have trespassed on our lands," the High Chief said accusingly. "The penalty for this is the Trial by Spears, led by the one who captured you. But Gallum is of your totem, and for him to cast a spear intending to kill you is forbidden."

Balulu said nothing, but his heart leaped at
hearing that he was not to endure the Trial by
Spears from marksmen such as these.

"So the Council of Elders has decided on another test," the High Chief went on. "You have
your boomerang, which you have told Gallum will
fly as far as a spear. Gallum will chose one spear,
and you will together hunt the great blue kangaroo. If Abishe wills that you slay a kangaroo before Gallum does, it will be a sign to us, and you
will be spared. If Gallum wins the contest, you
will be killed."

Another, louder murmur ran through the Council of Elders, and the group broke up, the older
members sitting cross-legged on the grass, the
younger ones moving away toward the trees. Presently some of them returned, weapons in hand,
and Balulu knew what they were for—if he lost
the contest.

Gallum now joined him, carrying a spear and
womera.

"Come," he said, and pointed down the valley.
Balulu looked, and saw, at the far end of the

valley, small groups of red and blue kangaroos feeding among scattered mulga and gum trees.

"We are to hunt together," Gallum reminded him, starting down the valley. "And do not try to escape," he warned, "for there will be sharp eyes and sharp spears all about."

It was true, Balulu realized, for along the slopes of the brush-covered hills that hemmed in the valley he could see figures slipping through the scrub. Now he knew where the rest of the young men of the council had gone.

As he and Gallum moved down the valley, only a few feet apart, Balulu considered his chances in this strange contest. Their hunt was to be for a blue kangaroo, he reflected, which was the female, more slender, faster, and warier than the heavier red male. Had it been one of the red males they were to hunt, he would have been more confident. He did not think Gallum's slender spear would have the power to kill a 200-pound male at the distance he knew his own heavy boomerang could. But with the more lightly built blue female, he was not so sure. He knew that Gallum's marks-

manship was as good as his own; he could only
hope that his rival would have to wait for a closer
distance than Balulu did to be sure of the kill. In
any event, he was determined to cast his weapon
before Gallum did.

As they drew nearer to the feeding kangaroos,
Balulu was overcome by a sudden sense of futil-
ity. What if he did win? The High Chief had
promised that his life would be spared if he did,
but the most he could hope for would be an un-
hindered departure from this rich, game-filled
land. What good would it do his starving people?
The tribe was too small and weak to drive out the
Valley People or force a division of their green
land.

Resolutely he stifled his discouragement. Tomorrow was tomorrow, and unless he concentrated his skill he would not live to see the next sun.
In that case the Desert People would not even
know that a better land than theirs existed.

They had now approached close enough to the
kangaroos to choose the object of their stalk, and
both veered slightly to the left, toward the near-

est grazing blue. They advanced slowly, keeping bushes and small leafy trees between them and the kangaroo they had singled out. They stopped stock still every time the blue kangaroo lifted her head to be sure no danger was near. She was grazing in a quartering direction away from them, alternately placing her short front legs on the ground in front of her, then pulling her great hind limbs forward.

Balulu was watching Gallum out of the corner of his eye. His rival had fitted his spear into his *womera,* but was not poised to throw. Obviously he did not think that they were near enough for either to risk a cast. Watching him, Balulu realized that two things were in his own favor. From his own experience hunting kangaroos in the desert, he had had to learn to kill at long distances, for there was frequently no scrub to screen his movements. Secondly, Gallum had never seen him throw a boomerang, and did not know how effective the heavy weapon could be at long range.

They were now within what Balulu considered possible throwing distance, but still Gallum gave no evidence that he was yet considering casting his spear. They advanced more slowly than ever and Balulu gave all his attention to a trained, critical judgment of distance, plus the direction and force of the slight breeze that was now blowing almost directly from their quarry to them.

The kangaroo raised her head, dropped it again, hitched herself along the ground, and fed. As he had been doing over and over, Balulu estimated the distance and the height from the ground that the kangaroo's head would be when she again raised it. Balulu tightened his grip on the familiar end of his boomerang, and tensed his muscles.

As the kangaroo lifted her head, Balulu stepped from behind a sheltering bush. Seeing him, the kangaroo froze for a momentary concentrated look at him, and Balulu threw his boomerang with all his strength.

The heavy weapon leapt from his hand, spun through the air, and arced downward, striking the animal squarely at the base of the skull. The kangaroo gave a convulsive leap and fell to the ground, its neck broken.

This time the Council of Elders sat in a circle, in the center of which stood Balulu and the High Chief, face to face. Outside the circle, but no longer tied, Warrigal sat on his haunches, panting gently, his bright eyes fixed on Balulu.

"Abishe willed it so," the High Chief was saying. "He strengthened your arm. He gave wings to your weapon. And since our legends say that his spirit brother is of the Dingo Totem, he must have guided you to us."

He looked around the circle, and low voices sounded agreement. Balulu glanced over the heads of the seated elders at Warrigal, who regarded him steadily.

"Since this is so," the High Chief concluded, "we will welcome your Desert People here. There is water and game for all in these valleys, and we will receive your people as brothers. Will they come?"

"They will come," Balulu answered.

ABOUT THE AUTHOR

JIM KJELGAARD's *first book was* Forest Patrol *(1941),
based on the wilderness experiences of himself and his
brother, a forest ranger. Since then he has written many
others—all of them concerned with the out-of-doors.* Big
Red, Irish Red, *and* Outlaw Red *are dog stories about
Irish setters.* A Nose for Trouble *and* Trailing Trouble
*are adventure mysteries centered around a young game
warden and his man-hunting bloodhound, who also appear in* Wildlife Cameraman. Kalak of the Ice *(a polar
bear) and* Chip, the Dam Builder *(a beaver) are wild-
animal stories.* Snow Dog *and* Wild Trek *describe the ad-
ventures of a trapper and his half-wild dog.* Haunt Fox *is
the story both of a fox and of the dog and boy who
trailed him, and* Stormy *is concerned with a wildfowl re-
triever and his young owner.* Fire-Hunter *is a story about
prehistoric man,* Rebel Siege *and* Buckskin Brigade *are
tales of American frontiersmen, and* Wolf Brother *pre-
sents the Indian side of "the winning of the West." The
cougar-hunting* Lion Hound *and the greyhound story,*
Desert Dog, *are laid in the present-day Southwest.*